Sitting Bull

Dakota Boy

Illustrated by Robert Jenney

Sitting Bull

Dakota Boy

By Augusta Stevenson

ALADDIN PAPERBACKS

First Aladdin Paperbacks edition April 1996

Aladdin Paperbacks
An imprint of Simon & Schuster
Children's Publishing Division
1230 Avenue of the Americas
New York, NY 10020

Designed by Antler & Baldwin, Inc.
Printed and bound in the United States of America
10   9   8   7   6   5

Library of Congress Cataloging-in-Publication Data
Stevenson, Augusta.
Sitting Bull / Dakota boy / By Augusta Stevenson ;
illustrated by Robert Jenney.
— 1st Aladdin Paperbacks ed.
p.   cm. — (Childhood of famous Americans)
Originally published: Indianapolis : Bobbs-Merrill, 1956.

SUMMARY: A biographical look at the childhood of Sitting Bull,
one of the greatest Sioux warriors to fight against the white man.

ISBN 0-689-80628-0
1. Sitting Bull, 1834?–1890—Juvenile literature.   2. Dakota
Indians—Biography—Juvenile literature.   [1. Sitting Bull,
1834?–1890—Childhood and youth.   2. Dakota Indians—Biography.
3. Indians of North America—Biography.]   I. Jenney, Robert, 1914–
ill.   II. Title.   III. Series: Childhood of famous Americans series.
E99.D1S6225   1996
978'.004975'0092—dc20
[B]   95-37306

To my Sioux friend, Mr. Theodore Le Compte, whose Indian name is Ooksheela Enockeeni (Running Feet). He belongs to Sitting Bull's tribe, the Hunkpapa Sioux of South Dakota.

Illustrations

Full Pages

Numerous smaller illustrations

Contents

Sitting Bull

Dakota Boy

A Strange Nickname

ONE SUMMER day in 1840 a queer thing was going on in a Sioux camp. This was in the Dakota Indian country. A young Sioux girl named Pretty Plume was trying to peep around her father's large tepee.

This maiden had reached her twelfth year. She was old enough to know she couldn't see around a cone-shaped tent, but she was determined to see who was out in front.

"Mother is there," she thought. "I hear her singing by the cook fire. If there is another person he is silent."

Pretty Plume peeped again. She had to know

whether her father were there. She stretched her neck, but still she couldn't see.

Finally she had to thrust out her head and look. At once she smiled. "There's no one else," she thought. "Yes, now I can tell her."

A moment later Pretty Plume joined the squaw at the cook fire. "Is Father about?" she asked softly.

"I haven't seen him, Daughter. Why do you ask?"

"I have something to tell you. I do not want him to hear. It would make him feel bad. It's about my brother."

Red Flower stopped stirring the stew in the large kettle. She opened her eyes wide. "What is it?" she asked quickly. "Is Jumping Badger in some trouble?"

"No, but I heard the boys call him that nickname again."

"The same name they called him yesterday?"

"Yes, Mother. Again and again they called him 'Slow'!"

"Perhaps you didn't hear them clearly."

"Oh, but I did! The boys were playing near by. It was a running game. Why, they even called Brother 'Slowpoke.'"

"That is bad. Your father will be sad when he learns this. He will think it a disgrace."

"I didn't want him to hear. I crept up and spoke softly," said Pretty Plume.

"Your father's enemies will laugh at him. They will say that the great buffalo hunter has a son called 'Slow.' They will say that the great warrior has a slowpoke for a son!"

"I was ashamed myself," the girl put in.

The squaw went on, "Some braves are jealous of your father, Daughter. They were angry when Chief Bear gave him the new name of Brave Bull."

"Father said it was an honor."

13

"It was indeed! It meant he was as brave as a buffalo bull and that he never ran away from danger."

Pretty Plume nodded. She knew about these brave bulls, for she lived in buffalo country. She had seen the great herds grazing on the plains.

Then her mind went back to her brother. "Do you have to tell Father about Jumping Badger, Mother?"

"Yes, he will have to know."

"He knows now," a deep voice said from the tepee opening. There stood the warrior and great hunter, Brave Bull. He was frowning as he joined his wife and daughter by the fire.

"While I was resting inside," he went on, "I heard your words, Daughter, and I didn't like them. My son should never have such a nick-name. It is a shame both to him and to me."

"It seems that he was too slow in his games," the squaw explained.

14

"He was a fast runner the last time I watched him. He could outrun other boys of his age. I have seen him beat his friends Wild Wind, Blue Horse, and Young Eagle. They were all a full year older."

Brave Bull turned to his daughter suddenly. "How long have boys been calling your brother 'Slow'?" he asked.

"I heard it the first time yesterday. They played near where I sewed."

"How did your brother act when they called him that?"

"He didn't say anything but his face grew red."

"That was a good sign. He was ashamed."

"S-sh!" the squaw Red Flower warned. "He is coming."

"Give him a chance to speak of this first," Brave Bull said softly. "We must not add to his shame."

"He doesn't come running as he used to," Red Flower whispered. "There is a change in him."

HE DIDN'T COME SINGING, EITHER

Jumping Badger came along the path slowly, so slowly the others noticed it.

"He's unhappy," the mother thought.

"He's lost his courage," the father thought.

Suddenly his sister felt sorry for him. She didn't know why. Perhaps it was because he was not singing. All Sioux sang as they walked along. Jumping Badger had always sung before.

Jumping Badger was nine-and-a-half years old, but he was as tall as a boy of ten. He was straight and strong. His dark hair was long—a braid hung over each shoulder. His eyes were brown. His skin was a reddish brown.

His family loved him dearly. They showed it now as they greeted him.

For the first time in his life Jumping Badger didn't return their smiles and greetings. He didn't even hear his mother say he was just in time for their meal.

"The boys made fun of me," he said. "They told me to go home and race with the girls."

"Did Blue Horse tell you that?" his father

asked. "Did Wild Wind and Young Eagle? I thought they were your best friends."

The boy shook his head. "I haven't been playing with them lately. They've gone to herd ponies out on the prairie."

"With whom did you play today?"

"I played with Red Fox and his brother, Sharp Face. I have been playing with them since the last full moon, Father."

Brave Bull wasn't pleased to hear this. "I am surprised," he said. "They have never come here to see you. Their father is my worst enemy. Did those boys give you this nickname?"

"Yes, they started it."

"Were you really slow, my son?"

"I—I—I guess so. But I'll beat them when I grow up. I'll kill more buffalo on every hunt."

"Don't brag," his father advised. "You may have to take it all back. They may become better hunters than you."

18

"They couldn't. Their father isn't a great hunter like you. Young Eagle said you were a famous buffalo hunter."

"Well, then, I should have a famous son. At least he shouldn't be a slowpoke."

"I won't be," replied Jumping Badger. "I am going to kill one hundred buffalo! I'll bring their hides back to show you."

"You'll be lucky to bring back your own hide if you don't learn to hurry," his mother said.

The others laughed. Then they ate their good hot meat stew and said no more about slowpokes.

After dinner Jumping Badger and his family sat around the fire and sang softly. Other families sang, too. The Sioux were truly a singing people.

Pretty Plume went to sleep. Jumping Badger blinked his eyes three times and then he, too, went to sleep. Their parents did not wake the children as they talked softly.

"There's something wrong with Jumping Badger," Brave Bull said. "I am troubled."

Red Flower had worry lines by her eyes. "Yes, something must be wrong with our son," she agreed. "He eats well. The trouble cannot be that he is hungry."

"No, our son is not hungry."

"Why don't you ask the medicine man?"

"The boy isn't sick. He is strong."

"The old witch might help him. She claims she can make magic."

"I know she claims that. I know she makes stews she says are magic. I've seen her stirring things in a black kettle when I have taken her meat," replied Brave Bull.

"You've been very kind to her. You've taken her meat after every hunt."

"It's my duty to help the poor and the old."

"I'm sure she'll help you. She'll want to repay you," said Mother quietly.

20

"Yes, I believe she will. She has always been grateful. I shall go to her now. The moon is high and I can see the path to her tepee on the riverbank. Don't tell the boy I went there. The witch might not wish it."

"I won't tell him."

Father rose and walked noiselessly toward the river.

The Witch's Cure

AFTER a time Jumping Badger woke up. Pretty Plume was already awake.

"Where's Father?" the boy asked.

"He went to see the witch," his mother replied.

"Why?"

"He wanted her to cure something."

"Was it one of his ponies? Did he tell you, Sister?"

The girl looked at her mother. The squaw shook her head. Then Pretty Plume shook her head at her brother.

"Mother, do you think the witch can cure horses?" the boy asked.

"It is said she can work magic. Why not on horses?" answered Mother.

"I hope she can work it for Father. I hope his hunting pony isn't sick. He's been training her for the buffalo hunt this fall."

The squaw had told her daughter. So now they looked at each other secretly. The boy didn't notice this and went on talking.

"It could have been his war pony," he said.

Still his mother and sister said nothing.

Jumping Badger gave up and lay down on his bed. "I'll sleep till Father comes," he said. "Please wake me then, Mother. I want to know about his pony and what the witch said."

He closed his eyes and tried to sleep but he couldn't. He was wide awake when he heard his sister whisper. He didn't hear her words.

Her mother didn't hear, either. "You can talk out loud now," she said. "The boy is asleep."

"I said my girl cousins were afraid of the

23

witch. Rose Leaf declared the witch made their dog disappear."

"How did it happen?"

"The witch was angry because their dog barked at her. She called out something and the dog ran away. It never came back."

Red Flower thought about this. Then she told her daugher, "The witch must have called out some very powerful magic words."

"Do you think she'll work magic on Brother?"

"She might. Your father will ask her to change him. He wants him called 'Slow' no longer."

"He went to see her about me," Jumping Badger thought. And he was a little frightened.

In his mind he saw the witch. Two buffalo horns were on her head. A buffalo tail was fastened to each braid. Buffalo hoofs were tied to her ankles. In the winter she wore a buffalo robe.

He remembered how he hid when he saw her coming. So did his friends.

Brave Bull entered the tepee now, but Jumping Badger pretended to be asleep. At once his father shook him gently.

The boy pretended to wake. He sat up on his bed.

"My son, I have talked with the witch about your slowness. She said it had been put upon you, like a sickness."

"Did she say who had done this?" Red Flower asked quickly.

"Yes, she named Brown Otter."

"Why, he's the father of Red Fox and Sharp Face!" the boy cried.

His father nodded. "And he is my worst enemy. He has urged his sons to call you 'Slow.' He knows that will shame me."

"Can the witch stop him?" the squaw asked.

"She declared she could. She said she would make Jumping Badger lucky in every way. He will be so lucky, I shall give him a new name."

"No one will call you 'Slow' or Jumping Badger any more," added Mother.

"I won't be called Jumping Badger any more?"

"No. But I must have some reason to change your name. You must do a brave deed first, my son. But just now you must go to the witch's tepee. Do you know where she lives?"

"She lives on the riverbank, but I do not want

to go there. It's dark under those trees. I'm afraid of her."

"She won't harm you. Go now and keep in shadows so no one will see you. The sons of Brown Otter must not follow you. Those were the witch's words."

Brave Bull opened the door flaps and Jumping Badger went out.

It took some time to get out of the large camp. However, the moon was still high when the boy reached the riverbank.

"I'm sure I wasn't followed," he said to himself. "No one was about to see me. Everyone was asleep. Even the dogs were quiet."

He wondered whether the witch had planned it that way. Suddenly an owl hooted overhead. "It's a sign," he thought. "She did plan it!"

He reached the witch's tepee but he was afraid to go in. "I'll wait a little while," he decided.

He looked at the moonlit water in the Grand

27

River below. He watched the ripples a long time. Still he didn't have the courage. Still he dreaded going up to that tepee.

Then, all of a sudden, a bony hand clutched his arm. It was the witch! He saw her two horns. He heard her hoofs rattle.

Her cracked voice spoke. "You needn't fear me. My horns will not hurt you. Neither will my hoofs. Your parents are my friends. Come along!"

The boy followed her to the entrance and inside. The witch pointed to a bearskin. Jumping Badger sat on it. She sat on another furry skin close by.

The door flaps were open and the tent was filled with moonlight. Jumping Badger saw the witch's face plainly.

"She is smiling!" he thought. "I'm not afraid of her now."

She began to speak. "You think you have no

enemies, but you have. They are Red Fox and Sharp Face, his brother."

"I have never quarreled with them."

"They have called you 'Slow' for a long time, haven't they?"

"Yes, I think so."

"I know so, for I know when they started. I heard Brown Otter tell his sons to begin this. I listened at the flaps of his tepee. A witch has the right to listen. You know that, don't you?"

"I—I—guess so."

"Brown Otter said you would think you were slow if they called you 'Slow.' He said it might take some time, but finally you would become slow. Do you understand?"

"I'm not sure——"

"You don't even try to run fast now, do you?"

"I guess I don't."

"You just let other boys win races and games."

"I know I can't win."

"That proves what I have told you. Well, I will change all that. You'll win from this time on. I owe that to your good father."

She stood up. She took a tooth from a bag around her neck. "This is a buffalo's tooth," she said. "I give it to you for a charm. I boiled it in my magic broth. I sang magic words while it cooked."

She motioned the boy to stand. Then she went on, "It will keep harm from you, and evil. Take it."

He took the tooth and held it carefully. "Thank you," he said politely.

"You must have it with you always," she said. "Wear it in a bag around your neck, or in one of your braids. Many braves wear charms in their hair."

"I know that. My father keeps a charm in his hair. So does my uncle, Four Horns."

"Every brave wears one."

"Will Sharp Face and Red Fox still call me 'Slow'?"

"No, indeed, they won't. You will beat Brown Otter's sons in every race you run. You'll throw them when you wrestle. You'll climb faster and jump higher."

"Ha, ha! They'll be very angry."

The witch nodded. "And so will their father," she said. "They may try to do you some harm."

"Won't the charm save me?"

"It will if you listen."

Jumping Badger didn't understand this. "Do you mean it will talk to me?"

"It will talk but you may not be able to hear its voice."

"But you could hear it. I could bring the tooth to you and you could tell me what it said."

"No, don't do that. The magic tooth will put words into your mind. They will be so clear you'll think they were spoken. Now, one more thing. Be sure to touch the tooth when you begin a game."

"Will it make me hurry a little?"

"You won't be called 'Slow' much longer. Go now, and quickly. The moon will soon be gone."

Jumping Badger put the tooth in his braid as soon as he left the tepee. Every now and then he touched it. All the way home he sang softly.

The Magic Buffalo Tooth

OF COURSE Jumping Badger's friends knew about the magic tooth, for he had told them. They were still excited about it, though another full moon had passed.

"Your charm is working," said Young Eagle.

"Look how you win the games!" Blue Horse exclaimed. "You beat Sharp Face and Red Fox every time. And both are a little older."

"I threw them both yesterday in a wrestling match," Jumping Badger boasted. "I wish you had seen them. They were furious. They said the tooth won the match. They told me to take it off and wrestle again."

"Did you?"

"No, indeed! And I don't intend to take it off. It's going to stay right here in this bag around my neck."

"Ho, ho!" the others laughed.

"They've stopped calling you 'Slow,' " Wild Wind put in.

"I noticed that!" Blue Horse exclaimed.

"So did I," said Young Eagle. "You're winning too many games to suit them. They'll think up something else to call you."

"Or they'll think up something to do against you," Blue Horse added. "You must watch them all the time."

"Watch them in every game," Wild Wind agreed.

"Keep a sharp eye in between times," Young Eagle added.

This didn't worry Jumping Badger. He was too happy to worry about anything. All the members of his family were happy, too. They held their heads higher and they sang oftener. No one could jeer at Brave Bull now because of a slow son.

One morning Cousins Rose Leaf and Little Bird came. With them was their father, Four Horns.

"We came to ask favors," the brave said politely. "We have questions to ask the magic tooth. Will you answer them, my nephew?"

"If I can, my uncle," Jumping Badger replied politely.

"Daughters, ask yours first," Four Horns said.

"Please ask the tooth where my doll is," Little Bird begged. "I've hunted everywhere and I can't find her."

"My question is more important," Rose Leaf said quickly. "I've lost my best moccasin. It was embroidered with beads and it was beautiful. Please ask your tooth where it is, Cousin!"

"My question is still more important," Four Horns began. "You all know that the Crow Indians are the Sioux's worst enemies. Our tribe has been fighting them for years."

"Brother, we have both fought them in many battles," Brave Bull said.

Four Horns nodded. Then he went on. "The Crows are determined to hunt on our land. We have scouts to watch for them, but they slip past some way and kill our game."

"They take the meat that belongs to us," Red Flower said angrily.

Four Horns turned to Jumping Badger. "Nephew, these Crows may be on our land now. I beg you to ask the tooth."

"Ask that question first, Son," Brave Bull said. "It is far more important than dolls and moccasins."

"I'll ask about them next," Jumping Badger told his cousins.

He took the tooth from the bag on his neck. He rolled it between his palms. Then he asked the question.

> "O shining tooth, I beg of you,
> Give me the words that
> I should speak.
> Put them into my mind.
> Are Crows hunting here?
> Here upon our land?"

There was silence. Everyone waited for Jumping Badger to speak. But he was silent.

After some time his father spoke. "Ask it again, Son. Perhaps it didn't hear you."

The boy spoke the same words again.

> "O shining tooth, I beg of you,
> Give me the words that
> I should speak.
> Put them into my mind.
> Are Crows hunting here?
> Here upon our land?"

Jumping Badger waited a moment. Still the magic tooth did not put words into his mind. It said nothing at all to him. Once again he rolled the tooth between his palms. Then he added new words to his question.

"If you are magic, let us know:
Do Crows hunt our buffalo?"

Again everyone waited for Jumping Badger to speak. Again he was silent. They waited and waited. Still he didn't speak.

"Are you sure you hear nothing?" his mother asked at last.

"No words come to my mind."

"I should think you'd hear something," his sister said.

"Maybe it whispers to you," Rose Leaf suggested.

"No! It does not whisper!" the boy cried sharply. "It says nothing to me at all."

"But it must!" his mother exclaimed.

"I think it does," his uncle said. "Jumping Badger doesn't understand how to use the tooth."

"That must be the reason," Brave Bull agreed.

Jumping Badger's face grew red. "You think it is my fault!" he cried. "It isn't! The tooth didn't speak. It isn't magic! It's nothing but an old tooth!"

He threw it down and rushed from the tepee.

Two Thieves

BROWN OTTER'S sons saw him leave. They had been hiding nearby, waiting for him to come out. They now followed him secretly.

They darted behind tepees. They crept around them. They hid behind bushes and trees. They sprang out from them. Jumping Badger didn't see this—he didn't even look around. He was too angry.

A group of Sioux girls noticed, however, and watched for a moment. "They're playing a game," one said. "The son of Brave Bull is the deer. The others are the hunters."

"They are stalking the deer," another girl said.

"I hope he gets away from them," said a girl named Pink Shell.

"But why?" the oldest girl asked. "Don't we want our hunters to catch every deer?"

"Not those hunters. I don't like them. Look how they sneak around!"

"Sister! That isn't sneaking! It's stalking! Hunters creep about when they follow a deer."

"Of course!" others agreed.

Pink Shell wasn't satisfied. She watched the two hunters until they disappeared.

She didn't know what their father had told them. She just had a strong feeling this was not play. She was right.

"You must follow Jumping Badger," Brown Otter told his sons only the night before. "Wait till you find him alone and take that tooth away from him. You will then win the games and races. You can call him 'Slow' again. Again his father will be shamed."

42

Presently the brothers saw Blue Horse join Jumping Badger. They saw the friends take the path to the river, and followed them. Then the brothers hid behind bushes on the bank. From here they watched the two boys below on the shore.

"They will go in swimming pretty soon," Red Fox said softly. "He won't leave the bag on the string around his neck. He'd be afraid of losing the tooth in the water."

Sharp Face nodded. "He'll hide it in his clothes. We'll find it."

The brothers waited some time. Then they became impatient. They decided the two friends didn't mean to swim.

"We'll have to take the bag from him," Red Fox declared. "You can hold Blue Horse, can't you?"

"Of course! I'm larger and stronger."

"I'll cut that rawhide string around Jumping

Badger's neck. Then I'll take the bag and run. You can follow me."

"You might cut his neck."

"It will be only a scratch if I do. He won't tell his father. He'd be ashamed to confess that I was stronger."

"I'm afraid the witch will find out. She might do something to us."

"Listen! I'll tell you a secret. I overheard Father tell Mother something last night. He said we would move to another Sioux camp as soon as we get that charm."

"Oh! Then she can't put a spell on us."

"Look! Blue Horse is jumping to his feet. He is pointing a finger at Jumping Badger. They are both speaking louder."

"Perhaps they have quarreled."

"It may be. Blue Horse is shaking his fist now, and he is shouting. Be quiet. Oh! Don't I wish I could hear what they say!"

Down below on the shore Blue Horse was really excited. "You threw the tooth away!" he declared. "You threw it away!"

"I was angry——"

"What were you thinking of?"

"I didn't think of anything. I was angry, I tell you."

"But it was a foolish thing to do! The tooth has brought you good luck."

"It brought me bad luck, too. It shamed me before company. My cousins thought I was to blame."

"No matter what they thought, you shouldn't have thrown it away. That witch will make trouble for you."

"What kind of trouble?"

"She could make you lose games again. She could keep you from starting on time."

"Well, I didn't really throw it away. I just

45

threw it down on the ground in the tepee. The bag is still tied around my neck. You see?"

"I see. I'm going after the tooth. Shall I tell your parents you are sorry? Shall I tell them you want it again?"

"Yes, yes, tell them that! They'll let you look for it. I'm ashamed to go back. My sister and my cousins would laugh at me."

"They might. Girls are awfully silly sometimes." Then Blue Horse hurried away.

Jumping Badger started to undress. He had taken off his shirt when he heard voices calling, "Hi! Hi! Wait! Wait!"

Sharp Face and Red Fox came running toward him. He thought they wanted to swim with him and waited. He had no thought of trouble.

Now they reached him. At once they seized him and held him tight.

"Give me that buffalo tooth!" Red Fox ordered. "And you needn't make a fuss about it, either."

46

"I haven't got it!"

"Oh, yes, you have! It's in the bag on your neck. Take it out and we'll let you go."

"Feel the bag! Then you'll know there's nothing in it," said Jumping Badger.

Each brother felt the bag. Each poked his finger into it. At last they were satisfied.

"There's nothing in it!" Red Fox exclaimed.

47

"Go through his clothes, Brother. Look well in his shirt."

"You won't find the tooth there," Jumping Badger said. He hadn't struggled to get away. He thought they would free him when they couldn't find the charm.

"It isn't in the shirt!" Sharp Face called.

"Look in his hair! Feel his braids all the way down."

"It isn't in my braids! Stop pulling them! It isn't there, I tell you!"

He began to struggle, but he couldn't get away. The brothers were larger and stronger. It was two against one, but Jumping Badger fought them fiercely now.

"I can't even feel his braids," Sharp Face complained. "He's swinging them about so."

"Cut them off!" Red Fox ordered. "Get out your knife! I'll hold him!"

"Help! Help!" Jumping Badger shouted.

"It won't do any good to yell," Red Fox said angrily. "There's no one about to hear. And stand still, or the knife will cut your throat."

Sharp Face had drawn a long hunting knife from a sheath of rawhide. He held it up. He seized a braid.

Now a man's deep voice shouted from the bank, "Drop that knife! Drop it!"

There on the bank stood Brave Bull! A gun was in his hand and the gun was aimed to shoot. The brothers looked and then they ran.

The brave came down the bank to the shore quickly. Blue Horse followed him.

"They wanted my charm!" Jumping Badger cried. "I almost lost my braids, Father!"

"I'm thankful I arrived in time to save them."

"Your father was looking for you when I met him," Blue Horse explained. "He had the tooth himself."

"I took it to the medicine man," Brave Bull

said. "I asked him what was wrong with it. I thought he might know."

"Could he tell you, Father?"

"He said there was no magic in it. He said the witch couldn't make magic. She just imagined she could."

"Oh!" both boys cried. They were both surprised.

Brave Bull smiled as he went on. "The medicine man declared that she wasn't even a witch."

"Oh!" both boys cried again. They were astonished now.

"He said she was just a poor old squaw who was a little light in her head."

"Then the tooth didn't win the games for me!"

"No. You did that by yourself. But the witch gave you the hope that you could win. We can thank her for that, Son."

"I will, Father. I'll take her rabbits and quail every time I go hunting."

Mares and Nightmares

THAT night Jumping Badger had a bad dream. He thought Sharp Face and Red Fox were after his pony. He saw them chasing her over the prairie. He saw them catch her. He saw a knife in each boy's hand. Then he woke up. It was a long time before he could sleep again.

Jumping Badger told his dream in the morning. His parents were troubled.

"Your dream could be a warning," his mother said. "Those boys might be planning to cut off your pony's tail or mane."

"Did you try to get to her?" Pretty Plume asked. "I mean, did you try in your dream?"

"Yes, I tried and tried, but something always held me back."

"Maybe those boys did cut off her tail last night," his sister suggested.

Jumping Badger's face grew red. "If they did, I'll settle with them," he cried angrily. "My mare has a beautiful tail and mane."

"Don't lift your hand against the boys," his father ordered. "If such a thing happens, I'll take care of them myself. I'll go to see their father."

"The boys will think I'm a coward."

"Then they must think that. I forbid you to fight them. You would lose. They are larger and stronger."

Jumping Badger did not argue. He gave his word that he would obey his father. Then he started to the opening of the tepee. "I must go out on the prairie," he said. "I want to see my pony." He left on a run.

He was almost afraid to look at the mare when he reached the prairie. He whistled, as he always did, and she came running to him.

"Oh!" the boy cried. "You've got your tail! You've got your mane, too!"

He threw his arms around her neck. He pressed his face against hers. The pony nuzzled against his arm and whinnied softly.

He went back smiling. "She's fine!" he told his family. "I'll ride her in a hunting game this morning. I told the boys I would meet them right away." He started to leave.

"Wait a moment!" his father cried. "There is something I must tell you. I watched your hunting game yesterday. I wasn't pleased with it."

"What was wrong? We were pretending to chase buffalo."

"You must ride harder and stop more quickly. Suppose a buffalo should turn suddenly and charge? What would you do?"

53

"I'd try to get away."

"You couldn't unless you knew how. Good hunters stop their ponies instantly. Then they wheel and ride in another direction. They must ride fast, too."

"I'll tell the other boys. They aren't herding ponies this week. We'll practice that, Father."

A little later four boys were galloping over the prairie bareback. They managed their horses with their knees. These were drawn up against their horses' necks. A light pressure showed the horses what directions to go.

Today the boys practiced stopping their ponies quickly while they were running. Over and over they tried it.

They would rest the horses and then practice again. At noon the ponies had a long rest. Their riders went home to eat. The boys needed a rest also. They had been riding hard for hours.

In the afternoon they practiced again, just as

long and just as hard. Jumping Badger was so tired he went to bed as soon as he had eaten.

During the night his parents heard him cry out loudly. They hurried to him and found him awake.

"I dreamed the same dream again," he said. "I was frightened for my mare. I was sure Red Fox and Sharp Face cut off her tail. I saw their knives."

It was the second warning, his mother said.

"If you dream it three times I shall go to Brown Otter," his father declared.

At dawn the boy hurried out to the prairie. He didn't even wait for his morning meal.

FOUR HORNS EXPLAINS

"The mare is all right," he told his family when he came back.

"I hope you won't have another nightmare,"

his sister said. "You scared me when you cried out in your sleep."

"I guess I was scared myself. I hope I won't dream it again."

But he did—that night! Again he saw knives held over his pony's tail. Again he saw the two boys who held them.

"This is the third warning," his mother said. "I believe those evil boys do plan to harm your pony."

"I think so, too," Pretty Plume said. "They're angry because they couldn't get your charm. They don't know it isn't magic."

Her brother didn't even hear this. He was on his way to the prairie pasture.

Then the warrior Brave Bull started to the tepee of his enemy, Brown Otter.

In just a little while Jumping Badger was back. "She is all right!" he shouted as he entered.

Then he saw his uncle sitting in the seat of

honor. This faced the entrance of the tepee. "Oh!" he cried. "I didn't see you."

"I don't blame you for shouting," Four Horns replied. "Your mother has told me everything. She has just finished the story."

"It won't be ended till my husband comes home," the squaw said sadly. "He might have trouble."

"There will be no trouble," Four Horns said. "I have learned that Brown Otter left in the night with his family. He has moved to another Sioux camp."

"For that I am indeed thankful," the squaw said.

"We all are. That man was a coward. He was also a poor hunter and a worse warrior."

At that very moment Father returned to his own tepee. "That is true," Brave Bull said as he entered. "You can spend all of your time riding, my son. Our enemies have moved away.

You may be sure now that you will have a horse, and that she will have a tail."

"Ho, ho!" the others laughed.

"The meal is ready!" Red Flower called. "I have roasted prairie hens in ashes."

Not many words were spoken as they ate the good food Red Flower had prepared. When there was little left but bones, Four Horns said, "I have been thinking about Jumping Badger's bad dream. Perhaps I can guess its cause."

"Tell us what you think. We are eager to hear," said Brave Bull.

"Well," began Four Horns, "what did Sharp Face and Red Fox try to do to Jumping Badger three days ago?"

"They tried to take my magic buffalo tooth," spoke up Jumping Badger, his face turning a bit red as he remembered.

"Yes, but what were they about to do to you when Brave Bull and Blue Horse came along?"

"Oh, they were just about to cut off my long, thick braids. They didn't care if the knife cut me, either. If Father hadn't come, they—they——"

Brave Bull understood the dream before Four Horns had a chance to finish explaining.

"Son, this thing hid itself in your mind. Each night you went to bed after playing all day with the pony you love so much. While you slept, some spirit so mixed these things in your mind that they had to explode in a bad dream."

"Yes, that is just what I guessed," said Uncle Four Horns. "Since we have talked about it, those memories will not be so mixed in your mind. You will have room for quiet, happy dreams again."

"I hope so!" sighed Pretty Plume.

"We all hope so," said everyone together.

Hungry
Grasshoppers

Four Horns turned to his nephew. "I watched you boys ride in a war game yesterday."

"Did you like it, Uncle?"

"I was disappointed. Not once did I see any of you take the side position. Not once did any of you cling to your horse's side while it galloped."

"That is hard to do. We thought we would try it later on——"

"No! Now! Every day! It is very important. Many Sioux warriors have saved their lives in that way. Enemies can't shoot them when the braves are hidden by their own horses."

Jumping Badger and his friends tried to follow Four Horn's advice. Day after day they flung their slender bodies over to their horses' sides. And day after day they fell.

They were still at it one morning after another moon had come and gone.

"I'm going to learn this if twelve moons have to rise and set," Jumping Badger had declared the day before.

His friends had agreed with him, but today they weren't doing well at all.

"There are too many grasshoppers flying about," Wild Wind said. "They bother me."

"They bother me, too!" Blue Horse exclaimed. "The air is full of them!"

"They're flying in my face!" Young Eagle cried. "Be careful! They'll fly in your mouths!"

"They'll eat every leaf on the trees and every blade of grass," Jumping Badger said. "Do you suppose they'll eat our tepees?"

"They couldn't," one said.

"They could," another declared.

"Well, they could try," said the third. "Anyway, they won't eat us."

"Come on!" Jumping Badger shouted. "I'm going back to camp!"

The other boys followed him. They found hoppers everywhere. Even the tepees were covered with them, and people were leaving the camp. They were going to the little caves in the bluffs along the river.

The boys started to follow, but they stopped

suddenly. Two medicine men were going toward the prairie. They wore their huge, ugly masks and carried deer-bone rattles.

Several braves and squaws followed them. The four boys joined this crowd.

"There's a new cloud of grasshoppers coming this way," a brave told the boys. "The medicine men will try to stop it."

"How can they?" a young boy asked.

"They will make magic. That will stop the insects at once. Watch! You'll see! The cloud will move in another direction."

The medicine men faced the cloud of oncoming hoppers. They shook their rattles. They danced, they hopped, they jumped about. But still the cloud came on.

The medicine men danced harder. They jumped higher. They hopped faster. They tried to shake their rattles louder. They shouted. They waved their arms.

But still the cloud came on. The next minute it was there! The sky was dark with grasshoppers. They dropped like rain from the heavens. The sound of their wings was like the roar of water.

The medicine men fled to the caves. Then the boys and everyone else fled. Jumping Badger hoped to meet his family, but he didn't. The crowd and the hoppers were too thick.

"Our families must be in caves by now," Blue Horse said. "We'd better find a place for ourselves."

Finally they found a cave that wasn't filled with people.

"Come in," a friendly squaw said. "It's dark in here. The hoppers won't enter dark places."

All day long the people stayed in the caves. The grasshoppers flew away in the evening. Then the Sioux went back to their camp.

There were no leaves on the trees along the

river. There was no grass on the prairie. The hoppers had eaten everything clean, but the tepees were still there.

Then squaws wept and braves were discouraged. "There will be no game this year," they said. "No buffalo or deer."

Then Chief Bear spoke. "My people, it could be worse," he said. "We won't starve. There is plenty of dried meat stored in the caves.

"In the years to come you will tell your grandchildren about this day. You will call it the 'Day of the Grasshoppers.'"

"I'd call it the 'Hungry Hoppers' Feast,'" Jumping Badger whispered to his friends.

Moving Day

THE NEXT spring Jumping Badger was ten. One morning there was great excitement in the camp. Tepees were taken down, dogs barked, and horses pranced.

Jumping Badger's youngest cousin was frightened. He was Pony Legs and he was only four. He had run off, but not very far. His cousin found him sitting on a pile of skins, crying.

"They're going away," he said. "They're going to leave me."

"Oh, your folks wouldn't leave you—they couldn't," Jumping Badger said. "Everyone has to go, even babies. Chief Bear said so. It's like this every spring, little Cousin. Don't you remember?"

Pony Legs shook his head.

"We move every spring. We come back in the summer. We move every fall. We come back in early winter. You know why, don't you?"

"Buffalo!"

"That's right. They won't come to us. We have to go to them."

"We go for their meat?"

"Yes, indeed! We go for their hides and hoofs and horns. We need every bit of them."

"Their tails, too?"

"Oh, we couldn't get along without their tails. The hairs make fine paintbrushes."

"I want a buffalo tail. I want to paint my face."

"I'll get some hairs for you. Listen! Your mother is calling you. Come along. I'll take you home."

Pony Legs was happy again.

Just yesterday two scouts had brought the good news to the camp.

"There's a buffalo herd grazing on the plains!" one had shouted. "Thousands of buffalo! Thousands!"

"Only a two-day journey!" the other had shouted.

Then the chief had given his order. "We will start early in the morning."

This meant everyone and everything. Tepees, kettles, clothing, bedding, horses, dogs, and pets—everything would be taken.

Jumping Badger helped his mother and sister pack their belongings. Their clothes, bearskin rugs, and buffalo bedcovers were tied in separate bundles.

The bundles were stacked in piles to be put on the drags in the morning. Drags were like large sleds. Instead of runners, two long tepee poles were fastened to a strong horse and allowed to

drag behind. Many bundles could be tied to the poles. Children could ride on the soft bundles.

At sunrise the next day tepees were taken down. The drags were made. The bundles were tied to the drags. Nothing could be left behind.

Pony Legs laughed as he watched people bring out pet skunks, badgers, birds, squirrels, dogs, and rabbits. He himself had a pet robin in a little cage made of willow.

"Do you wish to ride on the drag?" Brave Bull asked his daughter. "You can sit on the bundle of rugs."

"That is for little children," Pretty Plume replied. "I'll ride a pony, as Mother does."

"Then stay close to your mother. We may have trouble on the way. The Crows may think it a good time to attack."

"You'll be near us, won't you, Father?"

"I'll try. I'll be with the warriors riding on each side of the line."

"They ride there to protect the women and children," the mother said. "The Crows couldn't capture us without a hard fight."

"We are armed for that. Our scouts will watch for Crows," said Brave Bull.

"Where will you ride?" Pretty Plume asked her brother.

"Oh, I'll be with Blue Horse, Wild Wind, and Young Eagle. We don't have to ride in any one place. Our fathers said we could trot along nearby."

At last the long line of movers was ready.

The starting signal was given. A buffalo horn was blown loudly, twice. The line began to move. Almost at once the Indians began to sing. First the hunters sang:

> "We're coming, Buffalo!
> We come with bow and arrow.
> Don't run away from us,
> But turn toward us.
> Come to meet us.

Come to greet us.
Hi! Hi! Brother Buffalo!"

Then the warriors sang their song:

"Buffalo, you are brave.
Buffalo, you are strong.
You never turn back from danger.
Let us have your courage;
Show us how to face danger.
We would be like you, Brothers,
We would ever be like you."

Later on the squaws and maidens sang.

"Ho! Ho! Buffalo!
Hear the song of the squaws!
We need your meat,
We need your horns,
We need your tails and hoofs.
Ho! Ho! Buffalo!
We'll use every part of you."

The four boys made up their own song as
they rode along by themselves.

"Hi! Ho! Buffalo!
We sing as we ride

O'er the plains
For your hide.
Hi! Ho! Buffalo!
And we ride and we ride
O'er the plains
For your hide.
Hi! Ho! Buffalo!"

THE PEMMICAN TREAT

The Sioux never ate breakfast when they moved their camp. Their first meal would come later, when they stopped to rest their horses.

For some time Jumping Badger noticed that his friends kept looking at the sun. He knew the reason. He himself was hungry, but he wouldn't admit it.

However, he thought he'd tease the others a little. "You look at the sky so often," he said to Young Eagle. "What is wrong up there?"

"The same thing that is wrong down here. But it is a thing I won't mention."

74

—

"And why do you two gaze up so often?"
Jumping Badger asked the others. "Do you fear
a storm?"

"The storm is inside me. I won't even mention
the place," Wild Wind replied.

"I have the same trouble," Blue Horse confessed.

"Let us all tell the truth," Jumping Badger
proposed. "We are all hungry."

"S-sh!" Blue Horse exclaimed. "No Sioux would ever admit he was hungry, but I could eat a buffalo calf."

The boys licked their lips.

"I could eat a whole cow," said Young Eagle.

"I could eat a cow and a calf," Wild Wind declared.

"I could eat a tough old bull!" said Jumping Badger.

Then they laughed and held their stomachs. They made faces, too—terrible faces. They tried to see who could make the worst.

A horn was blown three times now. The boys stopped their nonsense. It was the signal to rest and eat. They rode back to the lines at once. Each boy joined his own family.

They knew they would have a cold meal. Kettles couldn't be unpacked. There was no time to spend on cooking. Hungry people were glad to eat the dried meat they called pemmican.

Jumping Badger was delighted with his piece of pemmican. "There's nothing better in the world!" he declared.

"You can thank me," his father said. "I shot the buffalo that gave the meat."

"Thank me, also," his mother said. "I dried the meat last fall. This spring I cooked it till it was tender."

"I pounded the meat after it was cooked," Pretty Plume said. "I pounded it to a pulp. Thank me," she added. "It was hard work."

"I picked the wild berries you put in the pulp," Jumping Badger said. "You can all thank me for that. The berries make it taste good."

Then this jolly family laughed happily. Each one asked for another piece of pemmican and got it. Every piece was eaten.

Presently the buffalo horn was blown three times. At once every family took its place in the line. There was no delay.

Warriors took their places at the sides, and also at the rear. The scouts went ahead—far ahead. They had to look out for danger.

The hunters didn't ride their hunting ponies. These had to be saved for the hunt. Young braves drove them at the rear.

Now the horn blew twice and the line began to move across the prairie.

Hunting Tales

JUMPING BADGER wanted to join his friends again so he rode along the line, searching for Young Eagle, Wild Wind, and Blue Horse. He had to ride slowly, for the line moved slowly.

Pulling their heavy drags, the horses couldn't run. They couldn't even walk fast with tepee poles dragging on the ground behind them.

These poles made dust, too. Jumping Badger was almost blinded by it. "I could pass the boys and not see them," he thought. "They couldn't see me, either."

Suddenly he had an idea. "I shall go hunting. I'll shoot enough rabbits and prairie hens for our supper. We'll have cook fires when we camp for the night.

"There won't be any large animals about. They will have been frightened away by the noise we make. I can shoot my game and get back before anyone misses me."

Jumping Badger had his bow and arrows. In a short while he had shot two rabbits and several prairie hens.

Some green trees grew on the bank of a little stream. As he rode in their shade, he thought how pleasant it was to be out of the hot sun. "I shall stop here a little and put my feet in the cool water of the stream."

He was so eager to cool off he forgot to hobble his pony when he dismounted. Soon he saw her far out on the prairie. The mare was too far away to catch. "She scented the other horses," he thought. "She's making for the cloud of dust. Oh, well, I can walk."

He looked about. It was very pleasant under the trees. "First, I shall rest," he told himself. "My people move slowly. It will be easy to catch up with them."

He lay down in the shade under a big tree. A gentle breeze was blowing and the birds were singing. Jumping Badger fell asleep.

A little yellow bird chirped loudly just above him. It made so much noise he opened his eyes and looked about.

"The bird is angry about something," he thought. "A snake may be crawling toward its nest."

The next moment he saw the reason. A big grizzly bear was coming toward the tree under which he lay!

"I'll jump up and run," the boy thought. "No, I can't do that. A grizzly can run faster than a man. I'll have to play dead, as hunters do."

Presently Jumping Badger smelled a strong

odor and knew the bear was over him. He heard it sniff at his face and body. He hardly dared to breathe.

The bear seemed to be moving away now. The odor wasn't so strong. He no longer heard its sniffing. But he was afraid to move for a long time. He feared the bear might see him and come back.

"I'll wait till the bird sings," he decided. "It is silent now." He waited for some time. At last the bird began to chirp. The boy stood up.

The bear had disappeared. Jumping Badger gathered up his game and started toward the cloud of dust. It was much farther away now. "I slept longer than I thought," he said to himself as he hurried across the prairie.

Soon a man rode away from the cloud of dust. He rode in the direction of the hurrying boy. When the tall warrior came nearer, Jumping Badger knew who it was.

"Here I am, Father!" he shouted. He waved and shouted again and again.

Brave Bull saw him and came riding fast. He allowed Jumping Badger to ride behind him on the strong pony. Before long the boy was telling his story. His father listened gravely.

"You were a brave boy," he said. "It took courage to play dead while a bear was sniffing over you."

Jumping Badger was pleased. "Can't you change my name now? You said you would when I did a brave——"

"Wait! You also did a bad thing. You left the line without asking. It was dangerous to stray away. You might have been captured by Crows."

"I didn't think of that."

"You'll remember after this. Your punishment will make you remember."

Jumping Badger was surprised. His father

had never whipped him. Sioux didn't whip their children.

Brave Bull spoke again. "This shall be your punishment—you shall not tell your bear story to anyone."

Again the boy was surprised. Every Sioux talked about his adventures. "Do you mean I can't tell my friends?"

"No, you may not tell your friends."

"Oh, Father!"

"Not one word to them, nor to your mother, or sister or cousins!"

This hurt Jumping Badger worse than a whip. To have been so close to a grizzly and not tell anyone! Why, even old hunters would brag about that.

"But, Father!" he began. "Can't I even tell the story to my uncle?"

"No—not even to him. I have spoken. You must obey me."

A TALL TALE

The Sioux made camp in the late afternoon but no tepees were put up. They would sleep in the open tonight.

Only Jumping Badger's family had fresh meat for supper.

"I'm glad you went hunting," his sister said. "This rabbit stew is good."

"There's nothing better than young rabbit," his mother said. "You have our thanks, Son."

Jumping Badger wanted to tell them about his adventure. But one look at his father's face settled that. He decided to talk about rabbits instead of bears.

That evening different hunters told stories around different campfires. Everyone went to hear them. Each chose the storyteller he liked best.

"Let's listen to Four Horns," Blue Horse suggested. "He always tells funny stories."

86

The others agreed. Then they squirmed and wiggled through the crowd around Four Horns. Now they were quite close, and just in time to hear him begin.

"I'd like to tell you about a bear I wrestled," he said. "I'm afraid you won't believe me. It's a very strange story."

"Go on! Go on!" voices cried. Braves winked at one another and smiled. They knew they would hear a big yarn.

Four Horns went on. "My brothers, I threw that bear three times."

"Ho, ho!" the listeners laughed.

"I feared you wouldn't believe me. There was a witness, my brothers. This witness was the bear's mate. That's right—his mate. She just sat down and watched us wrestle. The first time I threw him she growled fiercely. I was a little frightened."

"Did she show her teeth?" a hunter asked.

"Not yet, brother."

"That was lucky for you."

"Very lucky," Four Horns agreed. "She growled again when I threw him the second time. Still she didn't show her teeth."

"Some people are always lucky," another hunter remarked with a big wink.

Then Four Horns continued, "When I threw that bear the third time his mate was furious. She came straight at us, growling. And this time she did show her teeth!"

"Did you run?" a young boy asked.

"No, I didn't have to. She wasn't angry at me. She was angry at her mate because he had let me throw him. She boxed his ears. She bit his tail. She stamped on his feet—all four of them."

"Ha, ha!" excited children laughed.

"He got away from her finally, and ran. She ran after him. The last I heard, she was still scolding him."

Everyone laughed except Jumping Badger. He was thinking so hard of his bear story he forgot to laugh. "I wish I could tell them," he said to himself. "They wouldn't laugh at that. Not one of them ever has been so close to a grizzly bear. They would have bragged about it."

However, he obeyed his father and was silent. At last he left the campfire with his friends. They found a log near the stream. It was a good place to talk. He hoped they wouldn't talk about bears, but they did.

Young Eagle began it. "Do you think your uncle really wrestled with a bear?"

"If he did, it wasn't a grizzly."

"How do you know that?"

"He didn't say how bad it smelled."

"All bears smell bad," Wild Wind stated.

"Grizzlies are the worst. They'll make you sick in your stomach."

"How do you know so much? You talk as if

you had been close to one and sick in your stomach," Young Eagle teased.

"Ho, ho!" the others laughed.

Then, just in the nick of time for Jumping Badger, the horn blew once. It was the bedtime signal. At once fires were put out carefully. Every spark was stamped out.

The four boys said good night, and each hurried to his own family.

The Sioux knew they had to be up at dawn. In a few minutes they were asleep on the ground. It was a cool night but they were wrapped warmly in buffalo skins.

A Camp in Danger

THE SECOND day was like the first, hot and dusty. In the afternoon two scouts came galloping back to the line. They rode straight to Chief Bear.

"We have seen the buffalo!" said the first.

"It's a great herd!" cried the other scout.

Chief Bear told a brave to blow the buffalo horn. The long line stopped. Indians at the front of the line passed the word to those farther back. Everyone was excited.

"Hi! Hi! Hi!" Young and old sang with joy.

Chief Bear called for Brave Bull and some other warriors. "We will look for a good place to set up camp."

They rode their ponies beyond a pile of rocks not far from the place where the line stopped. Soon they came to a stream. It was not very deep, but it was fresh and cool.

"This water is clean. It should be enough for our people during the hunting season," declared Chief Bear.

"Few large trees grow along the bank, but there are many saplings. We will want those slender, young trees to make poles for the meat-drying racks. Also, we will want wood for cook fires," added Brave Bull.

"I saw berries nearby," said a warrior.

"The scouts saw small game in the brush. I think we will not find a better place to camp," put in another warrior.

"It is not likely that the buffalo herd will come to the stream at this place. It is too rocky. The brush is thick. Buffalo prefer the open prairie." Chief Bear wanted his people to be safe.

"Sound the horn," the chief told one warrior. "Bring the Sioux to this place beside the stream. This place will be our camp."

In a little while all of the Indians arrived at the stream. The braves took care of the drags and horses. Squaws put up the tepees.

The boys brought in wood for the cook fires.

"We will cook dried meat for the last time on this trip," a squaw said to her neighbor.

"Yes!" another squaw said. "Tomorrow we'll eat fresh buffalo steaks."

Then the squaws and small children went up the stream to bathe. They took plenty of soaproots with them. The men and boys bathed far below. They also used plenty of soaproots.

There were no stories this evening. Each tired family went to its own tepee.

"Tomorrow will bring hard work for everyone," Brave Bull said to his family. "Only papooses in their cradles will be idle."

"It is still light," Jumping Badger said. "I might see the herd. May I go out to look?"

"Yes, but don't stay long. You'll have hard work tomorrow, too. You boys must gather up the hoofs and horns."

"I'll stay just a few minutes." He went to the edge of the camp. He gazed out over the prairie. He saw the buffalo! "They're far away," he thought. "A mile or so, at least."

Pretty soon little Pony Legs stood beside him. He had run away again and his cousin knew it. "He wants to see the buffalo," Jumping Badger thought, and he was right.

"Where are they? I can't see them," the child said.

"Do you see that large brown place away out on the prairie?"

"Yes, I see it. What made the grass turn brown?"

"It isn't grass you see. It's brown buffalo—thousands of them, little Cousin."

"I wish they'd come closer so I could see them."

"No, no! It would be dangerous."

"Why would it?"

"Because they might become frightened and run this way. If they did, they'd crush everything. There wouldn't be a tepee left. Even the poles would be splinters."

"What would we do?"

Jumping Badger didn't want to frighten the child. So he tried to make it seem funny. "Oh, we'd just climb a tree," he said with a smile.

"I can't climb very fast."

"I'd give you a boost. I'd take you up high with me. We'd look down on the beasts as they rushed by."

"Ha ha!" Pony Legs laughed. Then he ran to tell his mother about it.

Jumping Badger hadn't laughed. He knew there were no large trees along the stream. He had been gathering wood there earlier.

"What would we do if a herd came rushing down on us?" he asked himself.

He asked his father the same question after he went to bed. He didn't get much of an answer.

"Go to sleep!" was all Brave Bull said.

THUNDERING HOOFS

There was no meal the next morning. No one had time to eat. The buffalo hunters left camp at sunrise. The other Sioux watched the hunters and the hunt from the edge of camp. Of course

Jumping Badger and his friends were in the crowd.

"Look at their ponies!" Young Eagle cried. "See how strong and wiry they are!"

"Hi!" Jumping Badger shouted. "Just watch those hunters ride bareback! They're wonderful! I wish I were riding with them. I wouldn't care if a bull charged me."

"You wouldn't have a chance," Blue Horse replied. "You wouldn't have the strength to shoot with those big bows."

"I'd use a gun."

"Only a few warriors have guns. The hunters all use bows and arrows."

"I shall practice till I can use them."

"You can't till you're older."

"I get older every day," said Jumping Badger.

"Ho, ho!" the others laughed.

"The hunters have reached the herd!" a boy cried. "The brown color is moving!"

"The buffalo are frightened. The hunters have killed some," an old hunter said.

"They are closer now," still another said. "A bull is leading them south."

"The herd is moving fast," an old man exclaimed. "Now I can see the beasts."

"Yes—yes!" others cried.

Suddenly a squaw screamed, "The bull has changed his course! He is headed this way!"

"The herd follows him!" cried another squaw.

"They come closer!" a brave exclaimed. "I hear the roar of the young bulls."

"I hear the thunder of their hoofs!" another brave shouted.

"They'll rush into our camp!" a maiden screamed with fear.

"They'll trample us and our children!"

Then there was great confusion. No one knew what to do. Where could they go to get away from the beasts?

Girls screamed. Children cried. Everyone was terrified.

Then two hunters did a brave deed. They rode out in front of the herd on their fast ponies. They took off their shirts. They waved them at the bull leader.

"Look! Look!" Jumping Badger shouted. "Are they trying to stop the bull?"

"Nothing on this earth could stop him after he has started," an old hunter declared. "They are trying to confuse him."

"Yes," a warrior agreed. "They are trying to turn him in another direction."

The people were silent now as they watched. They knew their lives depended on this trick with the shirts.

At last there was a great cry of joy. It came from everyone who watched.

"The bull has turned the other way!" a warrior cried to those standing further back.

"The herd follows him!" a brave shouted.

"Oh! We are safe now," a squaw exclaimed.

"Yes! Yes! We are safe!" voices murmured.

"I have never seen such brave hunters," an old man said. "They didn't know they could turn the bull. They were more likely to be trampled by him and the herd."

"It was a very brave deed," the chief said. "I shall give a feast in their honor."

The four boys were now more determined than ever to become hunters.

"Just think of them waving their shirts!" Jumping Badger cried.

"They were smart to think of it," Young Eagle added.

"I wonder if I would be that smart?" Jumping Badger said.

The others didn't answer. They were wondering if they would be, themselves. All four wondered about this for a long, long time.

Cheyenne Visitors

THE FOUR friends didn't meet often during the spring hunt. Each was busy with his own work.

One day there was a hard rain and all work had to stop. The boys met in Young Eagle's tepee. They had built a small fire and sat around it talking and bragging.

"I know I've cut down a hundred saplings," Wild Wind declared. "I trimmed them, too. Then I helped put up the poles."

"I know I put up two hundred cross poles," Blue Horse bragged.

"I've hung five hundred strips of buffalo meat on them," Jumping Badger boasted.

102

"I've hung up one thousand strips," Young Eagle joked.

The others laughed and he went on, "It's a village of poles. You can hardly see the tepees."

"There's enough meat now," Wild Wind said. "Chief Bear told my father that. We won't have to hang any more strips."

"Then we'll have to begin scraping hoofs and horns," Jumping Badger complained.

The boys groaned and made ugly faces. However, the next day they were scraping away and singing.

Soon after this the chief stopped the hunt. "Not another buffalo shall be killed," he declared.

In two days the movers started. A long string of pack horses carried the dried meat.

In two more days they reached their old camping place on the Grand River. Each family found the place where its home had been before the spring hunt. Each family put up its tepee in the same spot. Anyone could find his home on the darkest night.

Then everyone rested. Sometimes braves and boys went fishing. But mostly the braves talked about the buffalo hunt, and the boys listened.

One day visitors came. A Cheyenne chief rode into camp with ten warriors and their families. The men rode fine horses. Their wives and children rode ponies.

They brought their own tepees and food on drags. Their best clothes were in skin bags.

The Sioux chief greeted them warmly. "You are our tribe's friends," he said. "Your visit pleases us greatly."

Jumping Badger and his friends were delighted. They enjoyed playing with the Cheyenne boys even though the visitors spoke differently. It was not long before the Sioux boys learned Cheyenne words, and the Cheyenne visitors learned Sioux words.

"They like fun as much as we do," Jumping Badger told his family. "They like to wrestle, too. I threw one of them today."

"Did that make him angry?" his mother asked.

"No, he just laughed and wanted to wrestle again."

"Did you throw him again?" his sister asked.

"I didn't try. I let him throw me."

"Good!" his father exclaimed. "Visitors must be allowed to win some of the time."

"I DON'T LIKE THEIR GIRLS"

It was the third day of the visit. That evening Pretty Plume surprised her family. "I don't like the Cheyenne girls," she said sharply.

"Why don't you?" her mother asked.

"They made fun of our moccasins."

Red Flower was surprised. "What did they say to make you think that?"

"They didn't speak words. They just stuck out their feet and wiggled them. I knew what they meant. And so did the other Sioux girls. We let them know it, too."

"What did you do?"

"We pulled their moccasins off and threw them into the river."

"Hi!" her father exclaimed. "That was no way to treat visiting girls."

"The Cheyenne squaws won't like this," the mother declared. "They will think of the work it took to make those moccasins."

Now Brave Bull spoke sharply. "Those girls must have new moccasins. And our squaws must make them. We don't dare lose the Cheyennes for friends. We may need them to help us fight the Crows."

Red Flower nodded, agreeing. "They shall have new moccasins just as soon as we can make them. I'll tell other squaws tomorrow morning."

106

"I'll report this to Chief Bear. He will want to know. I'll go now to his tepee."

"I'm sorry I acted so, Mother."

"You should be sorry."

Jumping Badger tried to defend his sister. "I'm sure she didn't start it. She saw the other Sioux girls pulling off moccasins and so she——"

Pretty Plume interrupted. "No, I started it," she confessed.

Her mother frowned. "Go on. Tell me everything this time."

"A Cheyenne girl pointed to my feet and smiled. Then she held up one foot and pointed to it. The other Cheyenne girls laughed and she laughed with them. They were all making fun of my moccasins, Mother. It made me angry."

"I don't blame you!" her brother cried. "Our moccasins are prettier than theirs."

"They are made better," his mother agreed.

"I'm glad you don't blame me, Mother."

"But I do blame you. You did a very bad thing. You threw away moccasins that were not yours. The Cheyenne chief will be angry."

"I don't see how you got the moccasins off their feet. Surely they fought that."

"No, Brother, they thought we did it for fun. But they were angry when we threw the moccasins in the water."

"What happened then?"

"I don't know. We ran away."

"They must have been angry enough to scalp you."

"They did yell at us, but we didn't stop to listen."

"It's all bad," Red Flower said sadly. "It's very bad. And to think that you, my daughter, started it!"

"I'm sorry, Mother." The unhappy girl put her head on her mother's shoulder and wept.

Jumping Badger decided it was time to leave.

THE MOCCASIN QUARREL

The moccasin story went through the camp like wildfire. Even Sioux braves were worried. They talked about it together.

Would the Cheyenne chief take up this quarrel of the girls?

Would he order his people to leave now?

Would he speak at the big meeting tonight?

Young Sioux hunters joked about it a little, just among themselves.

"We should hunt on the water for big game."

"We should hunt moccasins instead of buffalo."

"Could you spear one while it floated?"

"It would be easier to spear a beast."

Certain Sioux squaws didn't joke. They were busy making moccasins for the eight Cheyenne girls. They had borrowed one Cheyenne moccasin for a pattern.

"Our work must be finished by evening," one squaw said. "The Cheyenne girls will want to wear these to the council fire tonight—if they go."

"Couldn't they wear their own extra moccasins?" another squaw asked. "All travelers carry two pairs."

"Of course they could. But Chief Bear feared they wouldn't come to the meeting unless we replaced their moccasins."

"The Cheyennes still might not come," another declared. "They may stay in their tepees."

"But the council fire is for them!" a young squaw exclaimed.

"Well, we will see what will happen."

That evening the large council tepee was

110

ready for the meeting. It was lighted by many burning torches.

The Sioux came early. All wore their best clothes. They were a sight to see—a beautiful sight! Doeskin dresses, deerskin shirts and moccasins embroidered with gay porcupine quills. Feathers, beads, chains, bracelets, earrings!

Then the Cheyennes came! They also were a sight to see. For they also loved fine clothes and jewelry. Doeskin, gay porcupine quills, feathers, chains, bracelets, earrings, and beads.

And every Sioux noticed the eight Cheyenne girls with their new moccasins.

Brave Bull said in a low voice to his son, "Notice the softness of the Cheyennes' doeskin clothing."

"It is no softer than ours."

His father smiled. "You must give some credit to other tribes, Son. The Cheyennes have as good tanners as the Dakota Sioux have."

"Mother said she would like to see the Cheyenne squaws' dresses."

"I wish she could, but she couldn't leave your sister. And Pretty Plume couldn't come. I wouldn't allow that. All eyes would have been upon her."

Now Chief Bear stood up to speak. He welcomed the Cheyenne visitors warmly. He didn't mention the trouble over the moccasins.

Next the Cheyenne chief spoke. "My brothers, we are happy to be here. You have made us feel welcome. And you, I hope, will visit us very soon.

"It doesn't matter that our children have quarreled a little. Should we go to battle because some moccasins have been lost? Shall we kill one another because young girls quarreled?"

"No! No!" the Sioux shouted.

The Cheyenne chief continued, "Besides, it was all a mistake. Our little girl wasn't boasting

112

about her moccasins. She held up her foot to show how small it was. Our girls are proud of their little feet."

"Ho, ho!" laughed the Sioux.

"My brothers, that is true," the chief went on. "Our women and girls do not work in cornfields. We haven't any. Our woman don't walk far because they have ponies to ride."

The Sioux nodded, agreeing.

"But our maidens found out something when they met your girls. They saw Sioux feet just as small as theirs. There are no cornfields for Sioux girls, either. Also there are plenty of ponies to ride."

"Yes! Yes!" Sioux voices cried. "Plenty of ponies!"

"And that was what the young Cheyenne girl tried to tell the Sioux maiden—that they both had small feet.

"There was no thought of moccasins in her

mind. So let there be no thought of them in ours. They are gone—they are floating downstream, like a bad dream.

"But our friendship is the same as ever. We are brothers still."

The Sioux were delighted. "Hi! Hi! Hi! Hi!" they shouted. And they sang all the way home.

Brave Bull and Jumping Badger sang louder than anyone else. They were so happy about Pretty Plume.

"She'll sing with us as soon as she knows," Jumping Badger said.

"So will her mother," said Brave Bull.

Stolen Horses

FALL had come and nights were cold. So were the mornings. Jumping Badger never wanted to get up. He was nice and warm under his buffalo skin covers. Every morning his mother had to wake him. This time she shook him—not too gently, either.

He awoke and sat up in his bed. "Why, it's broad daylight!" he exclaimed. "I told Wild Wind I'd be ready early."

"Then you mustn't keep him waiting. Your breakfast is ready. Dress quickly."

"I'll hurry. It's our turn to herd horses today. It won't be easy—there are so many new ones."

Red Flower nodded. "Chief Bear bought a large herd from the Cheyennes. They get them from the Comanches in that faraway southland."

"I wonder if I can herd them. I might let some stray away."

"I don't think you will. You know as much about horses as any boy."

"I like them."

"All Sioux boys like horses. So do our braves. They take good care of their horses. They keep them clean and healthy."

"That's the way I keep my pony."

"You grew up riding. You rode your own pony when you were only five," said Mother.

"That's why I'm bowlegged. My legs had to fit around the pony's sides. They were fat sides, too," he added, smiling.

"Your legs aren't bad. They're bowed only a little. Many riders have such legs."

They went outside. Jumping Badger sat on a log and ate a whole prairie hen. It had been roasted in hot ashes and was delicious.

Mother always had good things for Jumping Badger to eat. Everyone in the Sioux camp knew how well she fed her family. Other squaws would come to visit Red Flower when they thought she might be preparing prairie hen or one of her good meat stews. They watched carefully to see what wild herbs she would add. They wanted to please their families, too.

"Mother, do the Crows have as good food as the Sioux?" Jumping Badger wondered.

117

"I've heard they do not. There's not so much game on their land. It's rough and rocky."

As Jumping Badger finished the chicken, his father came. At once the family knew something was wrong. Brave Bull's face was red. His eyes were angry. "You won't herd horses today," he said. "The Crows stole them last night."

"Are you sure the thieves were Crows?" Red Flower asked.

"We found the prints of Crow moccasins. They have stolen our horses before, many times. This time we were lucky. We found five horses that had strayed away. I, with four other warriors, will chase the thieves. I came for my gun." He went into the tepee then, quickly.

"I hope they didn't get my pony. I hope she strayed, too," Jumping Badger said.

"I hope so, too, Son. She is a smart little mare."

Brave Bull came out with his gun and started away from his family.

"Wait! Here is some pemmican for you," the squaw said.

Brave Bull took the skin bag. Then he turned to his son. "Go out on the prairie with your friend," he advised. "Search for strays. Your pony may be with them."

Wild Wind came soon after Brave Bull left. The boys started out at once. There wasn't a horse on the prairie near the camp, so they went on.

Wild Wind's pony had also disappeared, and he also was unhappy. "The Crows stole a good pony when they got her," he said. "She was a pet."

"Mine was a pet, too. She'd come when I'd whistle and then she'd nuzzle my arm."

"It's a shame!"

"It is a shame!"

The sun was high now so the boys ate their pemmican lunches.

"I hope Crows never get this to eat," Wild Wind said. "It's too good for them."

"I hope they'll never have a chance to eat roasted prairie hen. That's too good for them, too."

"So is buffalo steak."

"So is young rabbit."

"They should eat worms."

"And snakes."

The boys laughed loudly at their own jokes. Then they went on eating.

THE BUFFALO WALLOW

Suddenly Jumping Badger had an idea. "Let's go to that big buffalo wallow!" he cried. "Do you remember that ridge by the hole?"

"Of course. That ridge was made by the dirt the beasts pawed out of the hole. Or perhaps they just wallowed it out."

120

"Father said it was both. Why couldn't we climb it? Then we could look far out over the prairie. And maybe we'd see our stray horses."

"The ridge isn't very high."

"It's high enough for that."

"It's a good idea. Let's go!"

They left the main trail and walked north. At last they reached the big wallow. They looked down into the deep hole.

"I wonder how many buffalo have wallowed here," Wild Wind said.

"It would take a good many to make such a wide wallow."

"And each buffalo wanted enough room to thrash around."

"They had to have room. They wanted to get rid of the ticks in their manes and skin."

"I wonder if we can climb the ridge," Wild Wind said. "It's pretty steep. The sun has made the dirt hard."

"Come on!" shouted Jumping Badger.

He scrambled up the steep ridge, and Wild Wind followed. Now they reached the top. At once they became excited.

"The Crows!" they cried together.

They hid quickly in the tall grass on the top. They peeped through it to watch.

"Look at that herd of horses with them!" Jumping Badger exclaimed. "It's our herd!"

"Of course it is! And those Indians are Crows. I can tell by the way they wear their hair."

"So can I. Do you think they saw us?"

"They couldn't have. They were riding away."

"You're right. Hi! They've turned! They're coming this way!" Jumping Badger cried. "Get down flat. Don't talk. Don't even whisper."

They peeped through the tall grass carefully. They saw six thieves riding toward them. Two others herded the horses on the prairie.

The Sioux boys knew many Crow words—enough to understand what the braves said when they reached the wallow.

"We'll stay here until our scout comes," the leader said. "He's spying on the Sioux to see if they are following us."

The men dismounted and hobbled their horses. Then they sat on the edge of the wallow and ate dried meat.

It was some time before the scout rode up. He reported to the leader at once. "The Sioux are following us. But there are only five warriors."

"They could put up a fierce fight. Some of us could be killed," a brave said.

The others nodded.

"Did they find our tracks?" the leader asked.

"No, the grass was too dry and the earth too hard. They just followed the trail to our land."

"They thought they'd overtake us before they reached it," the leader declared. "But we fooled

them. We backtracked on their own land. This wallow is in Sioux country."

"Ho, ho!" a brave laughed. "They'll never look for us here."

"They have turned back also," the scout said. "I think they have given up the chase."

"They feared to cross into Crow country with so few warriors," the leader told his men. "They knew our warriors would overpower them."

The braves nodded and smiled.

"Where are they now?" the leader asked.

"Not far away. Maybe two or three hours by pony. They have camped for the night. They're on the trail leading south."

"Then we'll camp here for the night. We'll ride for our own land at daybreak. Get your blankets from your horses. We'll sleep in this wallow."

While the Crows were busy, the boys had a chance to whisper.

"I'm afraid I'll sneeze," Wild Wind said.

"I'm afraid I'll go to sleep and roll down into the hole," Jumping Badger said.

The Crows came back with their blankets and guns. They climbed down into the wallow. The boys heard the Crows' voices but couldn't understand their words.

"Won't they ever go to sleep?" Jumping Badger wondered.

"If they would start snoring I could turn over," Wild Wind thought.

The boys were cold and stiff. They thought they couldn't stand it another minute, but they knew what would happen if they didn't lie quiet.

THE NIGHT-LONG WALK

At last the Crows slept. It was dark when the boys heard their heavy breathing.

Then Jumping Badger whispered to Wild

Wind, "I'm going to the Sioux camp on the trail. I'll tell the braves where to find our horses."

"I'll go with you."

"No, you must stay here. The Crows may decide to leave. You must watch the way they go. Our warriors will want to know."

Wild Wind didn't argue. Jumping Badger always took the lead. All the boys let him manage things. But Wild Wind did ask questions.

"How will you get by the herders?"

"I'll crawl past them."

"Won't you disturb the horses?"

"I'll watch out for that." Then he started down the ridge.

He knew how to climb down with care. His father had trained him. He went down slowly and softly.

Wild Wind heard only a rustle now and then. "It's not enough to wake the sleepers," he thought. "A Sioux knows how to be quiet."

127

The rustling stopped and he knew his friend was down. Then in a minute or so it began again. But in another minute he couldn't hear any noise. Nor did any horse neigh or whinny.

"He got past them," Wild Wind said to himself. "He got by the herders, too. If he hadn't they'd have brought him here to the leader."

Jumping Badger was safe so far. Wild Wind knew he was running along the trail south. The path in the starlight was easy to follow.

It was dawn when a boy stumbled into the Sioux camp on the trail. The braves were saddling their horses when they saw him.

"It's Jumping Badger!" they cried in surprise.

"My son!" Brave Bull exclaimed. He hurried to the boy and put an arm about him. He led him to a log and asked, "What has happened?"

Jumping Badger was so tired he could hardly answer. His voice was so weak the warriors gathered close to hear.

Brave Bull gave his son a drink of water from a skin water bag. Jumping Badger's voice grew stronger.

"Crows!" he said. "Crows with our horses!"

Then he told where they were and about his friend on the ridge.

"We'll be careful with our bullets," the leader said. "We'll all watch out for Wild Wind."

"In the wallow!" another exclaimed. "That's a long distance for a boy to walk."

"I walked all night. I ran as much as I could."

"You'll ride now," his father said. "You shall see us capture them."

"There is time for food," the leader said. "Here is pemmican. Eat it all. We will wait for you to rest."

"No! No! Wild Wind might go to sleep and roll down the ridge. Then the Crows would capture him. I can eat and rest while we ride."

"Very well, we will go."

Brave Bull lifted his son to his own horse. Away they galloped with the others.

Jumping Badger did see the Crows captured. Wild Wind saw it, too, from above. He didn't have to fear bullets, either, for no guns were fired. It happened quickly.

The Crows were still asleep in the wallow. They surrendered at once.

130

A little later the boys found their own ponies with the stolen herd. "Hi! Hi!" they shouted. "Hi! Hi! We found them!"

The Sioux warriors praised both boys. They said the whole tribe would be proud of them. They said Chief Bear should hear of Jumping Badger and how he had walked all night.

Brave Bull was so pleased he planned a feast to honor Jumping Badger. "After the fall hunt I shall have a feast for you, my son," declared Brave Bull. "Your relatives and friends will be invited. Then I shall change your name."

"Do you know what it will be?"

"Not yet, but I'm thinking. I want you to have a name that will tell the kind of boy you are."

"Oh!" Jumping Badger exclaimed. "What kind of boy am I?"

"Wait. Your new name will tell you."

Waiting

JUMPING BADGER hoped his father would change his name in the fall. The boy talked with Four Horns about it one day.

"Father promised to give a feast when he changed my name, but he hasn't mentioned it since we came back from the fall hunt. Do you think he has forgotten?"

"That is a thing he wouldn't forget, Nephew. He is very busy. He is showing the young braves how to train their ponies for war."

"There is no war now with the Crows." Jumping Badger felt sure of this.

"We never know when some other tribe will

attack us. We must have fast ponies ready. There's no better trainer than Brave Bull."

Jumping Badger was pleased. He liked to hear his father praised. So he nodded and smiled.

Four Horns went on, "His mind is always on his work. He'll talk when that is over. Then he'll give the feast. Your mother has already invited me and my family."

"I know, and she's making new clothes for me, Uncle. The shirt is soft doeskin. It's trimmed with colored porcupine quills. My sister has been dyeing them."

"I saw the dye pots outside when I came."

"My moccasins will be trimmed with colored quills, too."

"I am glad, Nephew. You should look fine at your naming feast. We'll all wear our best clothes. Your aunt is making new dresses for our daughters. She will make a new shirt for Pony Legs. It will be embroidered with red quills. His headband will be trimmed with glass beads."

"He'll be very handsome."

"He's been begging me to change his name."

"Ha, ha! He thinks he must be like me."

"He loves you dearly. There are many who love you. You have many friends."

"Oh! Mother has invited my three best friends. They are getting ready now. They'll all have new moccasins and new shirts, too."

"The feast should be held before the cold weather comes."

"Yes, indeed! There might be bad storms. We couldn't eat outdoors."

It was late fall before Brave Bull finished his work. Almost the next day there was a fierce snowstorm. Other storms followed with bitter cold and icy winds. This went on all winter.

Families huddled around the small fires in their tepees. It was no time for feasts.

134

So Jumping Badger was still Jumping Badger when spring came. He saw the new grass on the prairies. He noticed the new leaves on trees along the Grand River.

"I should get my new name now," he thought. "The weather is just right for a feast."

His parents began to talk about the food they would need for their guests.

"We must have buffalo steaks," Brave Bull said, "and moose and venison."

"Also baked prairie hen and wild goose," the squaw added.

"I'll gather wild turnip roots," Pretty Plume offered.

The very next day Chief Bear asked Brave Bull to lead a party of braves to the Cheyenne country. He was to buy a herd of horses there and bring them back at once.

Brave Bull told his family about this. "The terrible cold last winter killed many of our horses.

135

We'll need to buy a large herd. Your three friends will help to drive them back, Son."

"I could help them drive, too," Jumping Badger suggested.

"You're not old enough," his mother said.

"I'm almost as old as those boys. I was eleven this spring."

"You must wait till you are twelve years old," his father said. "Your friends are past twelve. One is thirteen."

"I can ride as fast as any of them."

"That may be. But you wouldn't have the strength to ride so long or so far."

"I'm pretty strong. I can lift——"

"Say no more," his mother put in. "Your father said you should be twelve."

"It will be a hard ride," Brave Bull went on. "There'll be no time for visiting. We must return at once. Chief Bear fears we'll have to fight white settlers this spring."

"Settlers! Here on the Sioux land!" Red Flower exclaimed.

"That shouldn't surprise you. They've been coming up the Missouri River for some time. There are several white settlements south of our land."

"The whites travel in great canoes," Jumping Badger said. "We saw one that time you took me to the Missouri, Father."

"Those are steamboats, Son. They puff and blow and make a great noise with the whistle."

"I'd like to hear that," Pretty Plume said.

"It would frighten you, Sister. It scared me that day."

"They shouldn't be allowed to stop by our shores," Red Flower declared. "Not if they carry white settlers."

"Chief Bear has sent a small war party to the Missouri to watch. They are to prevent settlers from landing. Or, if any have already landed, our warriors will capture them."

"Good! Good!" the squaw cried. "Whites must not be allowed to settle here and make their farms. They would leave no grass for the buffalo to eat."

"Then the buffalo wouldn't come to our land," Brave Bull said.

"The buffalo give us meat and clothing," Pretty Plume said.

"We couldn't live without them," her mother declared. "We would starve."

138

"I wish I were a warrior!" Jumping Badger exclaimed. "I'd love to go with a war party. I'd love to help capture the whites or drive them back to their boats!"

"You may have that chance someday," his father replied. "It won't be easy to keep them off our land. I fear we'll still be fighting them when you become a man, Son."

Missouri Adventure

Now Jumping Badger rode alone over the plains. His father and friends had gone to the Cheyennes to buy horses. He was a little lonely, but not very. He was working out a plan by himself. He was trying to see how much riding he could stand. Each day he rode farther.

He boasted about it at home. "I rode halfway to the Missouri River today, Mother. And I don't feel tired."

"That is good, my son."

"I may ride all the way tomorrow."

"If some white man doesn't scare you," his sister teased.

"If you see a white man you must hide in bushes at once," his mother advised.

"Should I hide from white men?" the boy said proudly. "I am a Sioux."

"Then try to act like one," his wise mother said. "A Sioux is not a fool. He never invites bullets."

The boy felt foolish. His face grew red and he stammered, "Oh—oh—I—I—was just joking. Of course, I'll hide—of course."

"You'd better not go to the river alone. The crews of those boats carry guns, I have heard. So do the passengers. There are always traders, hunters, and trappers traveling north. They will be armed, every one of them."

"Won't the settlers have guns, too?" Pretty Plume asked.

"I suppose so. They certainly know they can't settle here without a fight."

"I'll stay up on the bank, Mother. I'll keep myself out of gunshot."

It was noon when he reached the Missouri. He tied his pony to a sapling on the bluff. Then he went to the edge to look out over the river. He saw a steamboat tied up at the bank below. Jumping Badger's sharp eyes could see the passengers on the decks.

He found a shady place where he could watch the boat. Then he sat down to eat some pemmican. He forgot to look about, as his father had often told him to do. So he failed to see the two Crow hunters in the thicket back of him. They were eating pemmican, too, after a morning of hunting on Sioux land.

They crept toward Jumping Badger silently. They seized him and held him in spite of his struggles.

"A Sioux boy," one Crow said. "We'll take him back to our village. Our chief is always glad to get a Sioux captive."

"We can't watch the boy while we hunt."

"We'll tie him to a tree. Then we'll come back for him. Hold him while I cut grape vines."

Again Jumping Badger struggled to get away. But the Crow was strong and held him firmly. In a few minutes the boy couldn't move his arms, for he had been tied to a tree with strong vines. They had stuffed his mouth full of moss.

The Crows had just finished binding his legs when a bullet whizzed by their heads. It lodged in a tree back of them. Then another bullet lodged in a tree in front of them.

The Crows ran. A moment later Jumping Badger heard them ride away. "Who was shooting at them?" he wondered. "It must have been a Sioux warrior."

He waited for this warrior to come to his aid and free him. No Sioux appeared. Instead, a tall boy came along the trail. Jumping Badger was amazed, for the boy was white! He was the first white boy Jumping Badger had ever seen.

This boy carried a gun. His age seemed to be twelve years or so. He smiled at the Indian boy in a friendly way. "How-do?" he said.

Jumping Badger couldn't say anything, for his mouth was full of moss. He didn't understand the strange word anyway.

The white boy leaned his gun against a tree. Then he took the moss from Jumping Badger's mouth. After this he cut the vines that bound the Indian boy.

Now Jumping Badger was free. "You saved my life!" he cried. "I'll never forget that. Sioux don't forget such things, and I am a Sioux."

The white boy could understand only one word and that word was "Sioux." He smiled and tried to explain. "I was on the bank. I saw them tie you up. I came as soon as they left."

Jumping Badger didn't understand one word. He smiled and nodded and tried to show he was grateful for being saved.

The white boy went on talking. He seemed to think the Indian would understand. "I'm from the boat," he explained. "It had to stop here for wood. The crew has to cut down small trees and then chop up the trunks. That takes a long time."

Jumping Badger nodded and smiled. Then he smiled and nodded. He still didn't understand one word.

"So," said the white boy, "I thought I'd climb the bank. I wanted to see what was up here."

Again the Indian nodded and smiled.

Again the white boy went on. "My father is on the boat. He's taking me north with him to trap. He's a fine trapper. We'll get lots of furs."

The Indian wasn't smiling now. He was afraid the Crows would come back. He knew the boat passengers couldn't help them. They couldn't even see them. There was wide bottom land between the bank and the boat and many bushes. He pointed to them now.

The other boy thought he was pointing to the boat. "It won't leave me," he said. "I've got plenty of time. It will whistle when it's ready to sail. The captain said so."

Just then Jumping Badger saw a strange sight. A big wagon was being driven over a gangplank from the boat, onto the shore, and there were people in it. They were waving to the passengers on the deck.

The white boy explained, "They are settlers. They're going to farm here in this bottom land. They said they weren't afraid of Indians."

Now there was a loud sharp blast—the boat's whistle! For a moment Jumping Badger was frightened.

"I'll have to go," the traveler said. "The wood has been carried aboard. My father will be looking for me. Good-by! I'm glad I met you!"

Jumping Badger nodded and waved to the boy as he started to climb down the high bank.

The whistle blew again. Then a man ran over the gangplank to the shore. He looked about and shouted.

The white boy answered, "I'm coming! I'm coming, Father!"

The man saw the boy and ran along the shore to meet him.

"He wants the boy to hurry," Jumping Badger thought. "The boat is ready, and the boy will have to cross the bottom land."

Then came loud calls and shouts from the passengers on the deck. They weren't calling to the boy. They were all looking down-river. The Indian boy glanced that way, too.

The big wagon had started off across the bottom land. But now it had turned back. The driver was whipping the horses. He made them gallop over the bottom land and then along the shore.

After the wagon came the Sioux war party on

148

their fast ponies. Jumping Badger knew what they were trying to do.

"They'll try to get between the wagon and the boat," he thought. "If they do, everyone in the wagon will be captured. They'll be taken to our camp. Chief Bear will say how they should be punished for coming to Sioux land."

Suddenly Jumping Badger wanted the settlers to reach the boat. Then he felt ashamed of himself. "Why should I care?" he said.

But somehow or other he did care—on account of the white boy. And he was glad when the wagon was driven over the gangplank and was safe on the deck.

His joy didn't last long. He saw the Indians surround the white man and the boy on the shore. The boat crew and passengers didn't dare to shoot the Indians. They were afraid of hitting the trapper or his son.

The Indians put their two captives on an extra

pony. Then they rode away quickly. It was all over in a few minutes.

It wasn't over with Jumping Badger, however. He was grieved over the fate of the white boy. "That boy saved my life," he thought. "I wish I could save his."

A sad young Indian mounted his pony and started back to his camp.

Paleface Prisoners

JUMPING BADGER didn't try to overtake the war party. They were almost out of sight when he started. He didn't want to be with them, anyway. He wanted to ride alone so he could think things out.

"Chief Bear will punish the boy and his father," he said to himself. "The warriors will want them punished. They hate every white person. I thought I did, but I don't. I don't hate that white boy—I like him.

"It took a lot of courage to attack two Crows and then free me. Other Crows might have come up. He was as brave as an Indian boy."

A little later he exclaimed aloud, "I've got to save that boy! I'll tell Chief Bear about him. Maybe the chief will protect him, and his father, too.

"But maybe he won't. He might punish me for wanting to help a white person. The warriors would be angry, too, if I tried to save their prisoners. They think the whites will ruin our prairie and drive the buffalo away. Then the Indians would starve.

"I don't see how one boy could hurt us. He couldn't! Neither could just one man. I believe Father would say that if he were here. I think Mother would, too. I'll tell her about it as soon as I get home. She'll know what I ought to do.

"She has always told me to be grateful for any kindness, and to repay it if I could. Every Sioux is supposed to help his friends. This white boy is my friend—he did a friendly deed."

It was late in the day when Jumping Badger

reached the camp. He tied his pony and went straight to his tepee. He heard the news at once.

"We've got white prisoners!" Pretty Plume exclaimed. "Our war party just brought them."

"They are a white man and a boy," his mother added. "I think the boy is the white man's son. They look alike. I saw them as they passed here on the way to the chief's lodge."

"I saw them, too, and followed them," his sister went on. "Everyone followed them."

"Did Chief Bear speak to the prisoners? Did he tell them how they would be punished?"

"He refused to see them today," his mother replied. "A Cheyenne warrior was visiting him. The chief said he would sentence them tomorrow morning."

"I heard him say it. I came straight home to tell Mother," put in Pretty Plume.

"Where did they put the prisoners, Sister?"

"In that old tepee near the river."

"They could get out of that in the night. It's ready to fall down."

"They can't escape, Brother. Two braves will watch them. I saw the guards myself. I went with the crowd to the tepee."

"I wish I could see the boy," Jumping Badger said. "I believe I'll go to that tepee. I could peep through holes in the skins."

154

"Stay away from that boy," his mother said sharply. "Someone might think you were trying to be friendly."

"The guards wouldn't let you go near the tepee," Pretty Plume told him. "They drove everyone away."

"They were right," the squaw said firmly. "No Sioux should have anything to do with any white people. They'll seize our land as soon as they can. They've already seized land from the tribes south of us."

Then Jumping Badger knew he couldn't tell his mother about the white boy. He was even more sure after his uncle came a little later.

Four Horns began at once to talk about the prisoners. "One of the war party told me that the white man speaks our tongue. He claims to be a trapper, going far north to trap. He says his son will help him."

"He wouldn't say he was a settler," Red

Flower declared. "He wouldn't confess that, if he had a hoe up his sleeve."

Four Horns laughed and so did Pretty Plume. But Jumping Badger couldn't even smile. He was too worried.

"Maybe the man is a trapper," he suggested. "Father said there were always trappers and fur traders on those steamboats."

"Well, whatever he is, he's our enemy," his mother declared.

"I agree with you," Four Horns said firmly.

"Do you think the chief will punish them severely?" Jumping Badger asked his uncle.

"I'm sure he'll be hard on the man. There's just a chance the boy may be saved."

"How, Uncle? How?"

"Someone might claim him for a brother. That is a Sioux custom."

"A very old one," Red Flower said. "But I can't believe anyone would do that now."

"Yet it might happen. We need more hunters. Our braves will soon be too busy fighting to hunt. They must watch every good landing place on our land along the Missouri River. I heard that some settlers were driven back today."

"They were," said his nephew. "I saw them myself. They raced to get back to the boat. But this boy wasn't with them and neither was the man. That's why I hate to see them punished."

"Don't say that outside this tepee," his mother said sharply.

"No, you'd better not," his uncle agreed. "There is too much feeling against them."

A New Brother

JUMPING BADGER couldn't sleep very well that night. However, sometime during the night he made up his mind. "I'll claim the white boy for my brother," he said to himself. "I don't care if it does make some braves angry."

When he awoke, his mother and sister were gone. The morning meal was still hot in the kettle. He ate and then hurried to the open space in the center of the camp.

Prisoners were always brought here. Chief Bear sentenced them here. He told them the kind of punishment they would receive.

A crowd was there when Jumping Badger arrived. He was sure his mother and sister were in it, but he couldn't see them. He did see Four Horns and joined him.

Now the two captives were brought in by guards with guns. The crowd began to shout and yell angrily. Some shook their fists at the white man and boy. Some braves shook their hatchets.

Chief Bear came from his lodge nearby and the shouting ceased. But there were still angry mutters.

"Why are they so angry at the boy?" Jumping Badger asked Uncle Four Horns. "He has not harmed anyone."

"S-sh!" Four Horns warned. "Be careful what you say. Look at the angry faces around us."

"Do you think the chief will free them?" Jumping Badger asked after a moment.

"He wouldn't dare. If he did, he wouldn't be

chief much longer. The warriors would choose another. They are determined that these prisoners shall be punished."

"Uncle, I want to save the boy. Couldn't I claim him for my brother?"

"You could, but you'd better not try it."

"Why not? You said it was a Sioux custom."

"It is. But this time it couldn't be followed. The braves are too angry at all white settlers."

"Uncle, if I claim the boy, wouldn't his father be saved, too?"

"Now that I cannot answer, for I do not know. But why should you want to save this boy?"

"He saved my life just yesterday." Then Jumping Badger told how the Crow hunters had treated him.

"Why didn't you tell me this yesterday?"

"I was upset—I didn't know what to do."

"I might have talked to the braves this morning. Now it is too late. They are too angry."

"What could they do if I claimed him for my brother?"

"They could turn against you. Your own father couldn't save you."

"But if I could tell the chief what that boy did—how brave he was——"

"S-sh! Your voice is too loud. It's too late now."

"The chief hasn't spoken yet. He's just standing there looking at them."

"It's too late, I tell you. Look! Chief Bear has raised his arm. He will now state their punishment."

Quickly Jumping Badger rushed to the white boy's side. He took the boy's hand. "I claim this boy for my brother!" he shouted.

"Why do you choose him?" the Chief asked.

"Because he saved my life, Chief."

"Go on. Tell me everything."

Jumping Badger told the story. When he

finished, there were no more angry faces. Not an angry murmur was heard.

Then Chief Bear spoke. "This white boy has courage," he said. "He'll make a good hunter. He will live in the tepee of Brave Bull. He will become his son. The boy's white father will be released, or may become a member of our tribe also, if he wishes. We need trappers."

Now came an anxious moment for Jumping Badger. He ought to take his new brother to his tepee. But what would his mother do? Would she even let the white boy enter? And if she did, would she mistreat him?

He had plenty to worry about as he stood there waiting for his mother to come up. "The chief has consented," Jumping Badger thought. "Mother will surely do something."

Four Horns was telling Chief Bear that he would take the trapper into his home. The chief consented to this. The white man was pleased.

Then Red Flower came up quickly. She took the white boy's hand and smiled at him sweetly. "You are welcome to our tepee, my son," she said. "I am happy, for now I have two sons."

How Jumping Badger loved his mother for her kind words! His heart was so full he couldn't speak. He just took the white boy's hand and led him toward his parents' tepee.

"You have a brave nephew," the trapper told Four Horns. "It took great courage to face that crowd of angry braves and squaws."

Four Horns nodded. "And it took great courage to claim your son from Chief Bear."

"I believe Jumping Badger will be a chief himself someday."

"Maybe," Four Horns replied. "Maybe."

A Test of Courage

On the day Jumping Badger reached his twelfth year his father talked to him.

"Son, you have now become a brave. You will hunt and fight with them. But first your courage must be tested. This is the Sioux custom."

"I know it is, Father. I am ready."

"You must spend two days and two nights out on the plains alone. You must stay far away from the camp. You must not return, no matter what happens—not until the time is up."

"The afternoon of the third day," the boy added.

"That is right, Son."

"I can do it. I won't be afraid."

"You can't take any food with you. You can't kill game to eat."

"It won't hurt me to be hungry."

"Your hunger will help you to have dreams. The medicine man will come soon to explain that to you. He knows what dreams mean."

"What if I don't have any?"

"Then you'll be sent out again. Perhaps twice—or until you do dream."

"I want to dream of some animal."

"I hope you will. The animal you see in your dreams will bring you good luck always."

"I've heard braves say so."

"There are other reasons for your test. It is to see if you have the courage to take care of yourself while alone. And also to see if you are smart enough to stay alive. Wild animals may scent you."

"I'll have my bow and arrows and hatchet."

166

"Don't risk your life. You can climb a tree or run."

The medicine man now came to the tepee. Brave Bull opened the flaps and gave him the seat of honor.

Then the flaps were closed. Relatives waited outside. With them was the white boy. He was now called Come-on-Boat. He was as anxious as any Indian about his brother, Jumping Badger. He heard the murmer of voices in the tepee and wondered what they were saying.

"What does the medicine man say to Jumping Badger?" Come-on-Boat wondered about this.

Uncle Four Horns explained. "He tells Jumping Badger to be brave. Then he says magic words that will help him to be brave. The father of the family always helps the medicine man."

After a time the murmur of voices stopped. But the Indians knew what was going on.

"They are painting the boy's face and hands

and arms," Four Horns told Come-on-Boat. "They are making black streaks on them."

"Why?" Pony Legs asked.

"To keep evil spirits away from him."

"Will Brave Bull go out on the prairie with him?" Rose Leaf asked.

Her mother answered, "No, only the medicine man. He'll take Jumping Badger to some lonely place far away from the camp."

"Where is a lonely place?" Little Bird asked.

"Perhaps the river wood. Then the medicine man will come back."

"S-sh!" Four Horns whispered. "They are leaving the tepee."

The medicine man came from the tepee. He wore an ugly mask. He shook his deer-bone rattle and muttered magic words.

Jumping Badger followed him. He was dressed as usual. But there were streaks of black paint on his face, arms and hands. He looked straight ahead. He didn't speak to anyone. And no one spoke to him. This was the Sioux custom.

It was a solemn time. They all loved this boy, and he was going out alone to face danger. But his relatives were certain he'd be all right.

"He knows how to take care of himself," his aunt declared.

"Yes," said his uncle, "I have no fear for that boy. He has courage."

"Can't he eat anything?" Pony Legs asked.

"Nothing," his mother replied.

"He'll get hungry."

"That won't hurt him."

"Will I be hungry when I go out?"

"Of course. A brave has to learn to go hungry."

"Why?"

"An enemy might be following him. He might have no more arrows and have to hide. Maybe for two or three days he'd have nothing to eat."

"Or he might be following an enemy," Four Horns added. "If he should stop to eat, the enemy would escape."

"Oh!" Pony Legs exclaimed.

"Do you understand now?" his sister Rose Leaf asked.

Pony Legs didn't answer. He had turned to look at Jumping Badger. It was his last look, for his cousin was now entering the wood with the medicine man.

It was late afternoon of the third day. Jumping Badger's three friends were waiting at the edge of the camp. Come-on-Boat was with them. They had waited a long time. Now they began to worry.

"It is almost dusk," one said. "I fear he won't come now."

"I fear it, too," another said. "I wonder what his parents think? They stay in their tepee."

"That shows they are worried."

The relatives were talking softly among themselves. Every few minutes Little Bird would ask if her mother thought Cousin Jumping Badger would come.

Then Rose Leaf would ask her father what he thought. And Pony Legs would ask both of them over and over.

Finally their mother stopped the questions. "He will come," she said firmly.

171

"Of course," their father agreed. "No one has to worry about that boy."

"May I go to meet him?" Pony Legs asked his father.

"No, Son. Stay here by my side. No one will go to meet him. That is our custom."

Nearby a group of Indian maidens talked together softly.

"Perhaps he is ashamed to come in daylight," one said. "Perhaps he will wait till dark."

The others were surprised. "Why should he be ashamed?" they asked.

"Maybe someone took him food and he ate it."

"Do you mean that someone may have tried to tempt him?" another asked.

"That has been done before to others."

"But who would do such a thing to Jumping Badger? Everyone likes him."

"Someone who liked him would do it. It would give him a chance to show his courage."

172

"By refusing to eat?"

"Yes."

"Do you think his uncle would tempt him?"

"He might. Or maybe the medicine man himself."

"There comes Jumping Badger!" Blue Horse cried.

"Hi! He comes!" Young Eagle shouted.

"Look!" Wild Wind cried. "He has killed a deer. He is carrying it on his back!"

Jumping Badger smiled now and waved his hand. But he didn't stop to speak with anyone—not even with his relatives or best friends. He went straight to his father's tepee. He entered it alone.

His mother gave him a little food. "It won't do to eat too much at first," she said.

Then he told his dreams. "I dreamed I was hunting buffalo. I shot at a bull and hit it. Then I saw the bull sit down."

"Buffalo don't sit," his sister put in.

"They do when they are wounded in their hind legs," her father explained. "They can't stand—they're obliged to sit."

"That isn't all," the boy went on. "I saw many bulls. They were thick about me. Every one was sitting down."

"Hi!" his father exclaimed. "I can tell you what that means. We needn't wait for the medicine man."

"Was it a good dream?"

"It was very good. You couldn't have had a better one. You'll be a great buffalo hunter. Your arrows will cause a thousand bulls to sit. Now I can give you your new name. From this day on you shall be called Sitting Bull. May the name bring you honor always!"

Then he took his son's hand and led him from the tepee. Red Flower and Pretty Plume followed. They were proud of Jumping Badger.

Now Brave Bull told the waiting relatives and friends about his son's new name. All were pleased.

"Hi! Hi!" cried the relatives.

"Hi! Hi!" cried the friends.

"Hi! Hi! Sitting Bull! Hi!" they all cried.

Then they all sat down together to the feast which they had begun to plan long ago.

Chief Sitting Bull

MANY years passed. The boy Sitting Bull was now a brave and a great hunter. There was none better in his Sioux tribe. Everyone praised him.

"He has the right name," other hunters agreed. "He makes bulls sit on every hunt."

The squaws were thankful to him. "We know our children won't go hungry now," they said. "We know we'll all have meat as long as Sitting Bull hunts."

The warriors admired him because he was brave. "He never runs away from danger," they said. "He is indeed like a buffalo. He'll charge his enemy even if it's a grizzly bear."

The old people had good reason to think well of him. "He never forgets to bring us meat," they said.

The young people liked Sitting Bull because he played games with them and watched their pony races.

"He praises us all for trying to win," they told their parents.

The children loved him because he told them funny stories about animals. Sometimes he made up songs and sang to them.

It was no wonder Sitting Bull was made chief when the old chief died. The warriors put a beautiful bonnet of eagle feathers on his head. They gave him their finest and swiftest horse to ride.

One year later Warrior Red Cloud spoke to other warriors. "We made no mistake when we selected Sitting Bull for our chief," he declared. "We have never been so lucky."

Warrior Spotted Tail agreed with him. "Look how Sitting Bull got rid of enemy hunters," he said. "No tribe dares to hunt on our land now."

Then Warrior Crazy Horse spoke. "Look how he has had to fight white settlers. And look how he has kept them away. The other Plains tribes have many settlements."

"Yes," said Red Cloud. "Their chiefs couldn't push the whites back."

179

All the Sioux were pleased. They thought these good times would last. Then numbers of white hunters came to the Great Plains. They killed buffalo by the thousands. They killed for the hides, for these brought a good price in cities.

The Great Plains were so very great that it was impossible to watch everywhere. Even Sitting Bull's warriors couldn't stop this killing.

So it became harder for the Sioux hunters to find enough buffalo for meat. There was much grumbling now among the people. Sometimes there was hunger.

GOLD IN THE BLACK HILLS

One day two Indian scouts hurried to the tepee of Chief Sitting Bull. Many braves and squaws followed. There would be news and they wanted to hear it.

The chief talked with the scouts outside. "Your news is bad," he said. "I see it in your faces. Speak! Keep nothing from my ears."

"There is trouble in our Black Hills," one began. "Gold has been discovered there."

"We discovered it long ago," Chief Sitting Bull replied. "We have used a little for our jewelry, but we have never mined it. What is this trouble?"

"White men have found the gold, Chief. The news has spread like a prairie fire. Hundreds of whites have come to those hills to dig."

"Many more are on the way," the other scout added. "They come up the Missouri by steamboat. From there they come by wagon, mule and horse. Some walk. All race to get to the gold diggings first."

"Does it seem that the white strangers plan to stay long?" Sitting Bull wanted to know.

"Yes, Chief, some families have come already."

The chief's face had grown angry. "Those hills belong to us," he said. "They belonged to our grandfathers and to their fathers. Our medicine men climb them to be nearer to the Great Spirit."

The people nodded gravely.

"I myself have climbed them to pray to Him."

Again the people nodded gravely.

The chief went on, "No white man has the right to dig for gold there. We'll not allow it."

"Hi! Hi!" the people cried. Everyone agreed with the chief.

Now he told them more. "Our white Grandfather, the President in Washington, told us that no other feet than ours should ever walk there. That is written down on paper."

"Has the Grandfather forgotten his promise?" Crazy Horse asked.

"I think he has," Sitting Bull replied. "Or those miners wouldn't be here."

"Or else they are crazed by the thought of gold," Red Cloud suggested.

"No matter how it happened!" Sitting Bull cried. "They must be driven out!"

"Yes! Yes!" the people cried.

"Are these miners armed?" the chief asked the scouts.

"Every man carries a gun, Chief, but that is

183

not all the trouble. Soldiers have come to protect them. A soldiers' fort has been built nearby."

Warriors and braves now shouted angrily.

"You see? The Grandfather hasn't kept his promise," Chief Sitting Bull told them. "We'll destroy the fort! We'll drive the soldiers out with the miners!"

"Yes! Yes!" the others shouted.

The chief raised his arm. There was silence, and then he spoke. "This means war. I'll call the warriors from every Sioux camp in this country. I'll send runners at once. And you yourselves are to get ready."

THE GRANDFATHER SPEAKS

Two years later President Grant held a meeting of army officers at the White House in Washington.

"Gentlemen," the President began, "I've had

184

very bad news from the western Plains. Chief Sitting Bull has defeated General George Custer and his cavalry. The general made his last stand on the Little Big Horn River in Montana."

The officers were amazed.

"Defeated General Custer!" one exclaimed. "He was one of the best officers in the army."

"He made a great mistake. He thought Sitting Bull had a small force of warriors. He marched against the Indians with only some two hundred cavalrymen.

"His troops were surrounded by a large force of warriors. There were between two and three thousand. Every white man was killed."

"That is indeed bad news," an officer said.

The President went on: "The settlers in the West are alarmed. They fear Sitting Bull will attack the settlements next. They have written me for help."

"The army has built several forts out there,"

a colonel said. "For years we've been sending troops there. Why can't they protect the settlers?"

"Because Chief Sitting Bull outsmarts them," President Grant replied. "He seems to be the victor in every fight."

"If he is so smart why doesn't he see the mistake he is making?" another officer asked. "He is preventing the Plains from being settled."

"He doesn't want them settled," the President explained. "He thinks the Great Spirit put the Sioux on the Plains and gave them wild animals to hunt."

"Towns and cities could be built there," still another officer said. "There is room for thousands of farms. Instead, a few savages want it all for themselves and wild animals."

"Chief Sitting Bull should persuade his people to farm and raise their own food," a general stated. "He should be glad to see them in com-

186

fortable houses. He should be happy to see the children going to school."

"I've tried to persuade him," the President said. "I sent an officer to him under a flag of truce. Sitting Bull treated this man politely and listened to his words.

"Then the chief replied. He said the Great Spirit had made the Sioux Indians. And He expected them to live like Indians."

"Do you think he really believed that?"

"Yes, Major, I do. The officer said he did. Sitting Bull is devoted to his people. But it is impossible for him to see with the white man's eyes, or to think with the white man's mind."

"He'll never change," the colonel said.

"He must be forced to change. Nothing can be done this winter. But when spring comes I propose to send a big army against his forces. It is time that part of the United States was ruled by our government."

"Yes! Yes!" the others agreed. "The United States must take action against the Sioux."

IN THE SIOUX CAMP

A change had come over Sitting Bull's Sioux. They no longer boasted of their victories over the whites. They were tired of fighting.

Red Cloud told the chief about this. "They have lost too many sons in battle."

"Do they wish me to make peace with the white enemy?"

"They said the other Plains tribes had made peace with the whites."

"If they had listened to me, they would have no white settlements now. I tried to unite the tribes. But their chiefs were afraid, like old squaws."

"They are trying to farm and live like whites."

"No white man will ever put a hoe in my hand. They shall not force my people to farm!"

188

Then Spotted Tail went to the chief's tepee. "I speak for peace," he said. "It is no use to fight the white men. There are too many of them. I have been to Washington—I know."

"You listened to the Grandfather's words," Sitting Bull replied.

"No, I saw with my own eyes. The whites are too strong for us."

"I'll never let my people become their slaves."

"The Grandfather said we would be free men."

"I can't believe his words. No! We will fight on."

Crazy Horse talked with the chief next. "The Grandfather has offered us many things if we will make peace," he said. "There will be houses and schools."

"We teach our children all they have to know. And we do not need their houses."

"The Grandfather will send a great army here.

190

It will be greater than any that has come before. We can't fight their cannon."

"I'll never surrender to them. Never!"

"Then we go on fighting?"

"Yes! As long as there is one Sioux to bear a gun."

But that year another enemy crept up on the Sioux. This new enemy was starvation. Chief Sitting Bull couldn't fight it. The herds of buffalo were gone. There wasn't enough small game. His people fell ill from lack of food. Little children were dying.

Chief Sitting Bull's heart was broken. He loved his people. He couldn't bear to see them suffer. So one day he rode to an army fort and asked to see the commander.

"I do not bear a flag of truce," he said. "I have come to surrender. I beg you to feed my starving people."

"We'll feed every hungry Sioux," the commander promised. "And you yourself shall be pardoned. The Grandfather has so spoken."

"He will not punish me?" the chief asked with surprise.

"No. He knows you thought only of your people. You fought for what you thought was right. Go back to your camp and rest in peace."